Love yo
Hate yo
Just do
know

Are you in a world where parents always "know what is best for you", brothers and sisters are as sensitive as Attila the Hun, teachers would be more at home in a lunatic asylum, and friends — well — who needs them anyway?

Surprisingly in this grim scene there are a few understanding people who know what it's all about. To find out who they are and where to find them — read on ...

This collection includes stories by
> **Rosamunde Blackler**
> **Petronella Breinburg**
> **Freda Kelsall**
> **Sam McBratney**
> **Jan Mark**
> **Joan Salvesen**
> **Marion Rachel Stewart**
> **Mary Sullivan**
> **Robert Westall**
> **Kenneth Wood**

Love you, Hate you, Just don't know

Hippo Books
Scholastic Publications Limited
London

Scholastic Publications Ltd, 141–143 Drury Lane,
London WC2

Scholastic Book Services, 50 West 44th Street,
New York NY 10036 USA

Scholastic Tab Publications Ltd, 123 Newkirk Road,
Richmond Hill, Ontario L4C 3G5 Canada

H J Ashton Co Pty Ltd, Box 579, Gosford,
New South Wales, Australia

H J Ashton Co Pty Ltd, 9–11 Fairfax Avenue,
Penrose, Auckland, New Zealand

First published by Evans Brothers Ltd 1980
Published by Scholastic Publications Ltd 1981
This selection © 1980 Evans Brothers Ltd
The copyright of each story remains the property of the
author
All rights reserved

Typeset by Computacomp (UK) Ltd, Fort William, Scotland
Made and printed in the USA

CONTENTS

FEET

Jan Mark

Unlike the Centre Court at Wimbledon, the Centre
Court at our school is the one nobody wants to play
on. It is made of asphalt and has dents in it, like
Ryvita. All the other courts are grass, out in the sun;
Centre Court is in between the science block and the
canteen and when there is a Governors' Meeting the
governors use it as a car park. The sun only shines on
Centre Court at noon in June and there is green algae
growing round the edges. When I volunteered to be
an umpire at the annual tennis tournament I might
have known that I was going to end up on Centre
Court.

"You'd better go on Centre Court," said Mr
Evans, "as it's your first time. It won't matter so
much if you make mistakes." I love Mr Evans. He is
so tactful and he looks like an orang-utan in his track
suit. I believe myself that he swings from the pipes in
the changing room, but I haven't personally observed
this, you understand. He just looks as if he might
enjoy swinging from things. He has very long arms.
Probably he can peel bananas with his toes, which
have little tufts of hair on, like beard transplants. I
saw them once.

So I was sitting up in my umpire's chair, just like
Wimbledon, with an official school pencil and a pad
of score cards and I wasn't making any mistakes.
This was mainly because they were all first round
matches, the six love, six love kind, to get rid of the

I

worst players. All my matches were ladies' doubles which is what you call the fifth and sixth year girls when they are playing tennis although not at any other time. We didn't get any spectators except some first year boys who came to look at the legs and things and Mr Evans, on and off, who was probably there for the same reason.

All the men's matches were on the grass courts, naturally, so I didn't see what I wanted to see which was Michael Collier. I suppose it was the thought of umpiring Collier that made me put my name down in the first place, before I remembered about ending up on Centre Court. I could only hope that I would be finished in time for the Men's Final so that I could go and watch it because Collier would definitely be in the final. People said that it was hardly worth his while playing, really, why didn't they just give him the trophy and have done with it?

Looking back, I dare say that's what he thought, too.

So anyway, I got rid of all my ladies' doubles and sat around waiting for a mixed doubles. It was cold and windy on Centre Court since it wasn't noon in June, and I wished I had worn a sweater instead of trying to look attractive sort of in short sleeves. Sort of is right. That kind of thing doesn't fool anyone. I had these sandals too which let the draught in something rotten. I should have worn wellies. No one would have noticed. Nobody looks at feet.

After the mixed doubles which was a fiasco I thought of going in to get a hot drink – tea or coffee or just boiling water would have done – when I noticed this thing coming down the tramlines and trying to walk on one leg like Richard the Third only all in white.

Richard the Bride.

It was using a tennis racquet head-down as a

walking stick which is not done, like cheating at cards. No gentleman would do this to his tennis racquet. This is no gentleman.

"Ho," says this Richard the Third person. "Me Carson. You Jane."

This does not quite qualify as Pun of the Week because he *is* Carson and I *am* Jane. He is Alan Carson from the sixth form — only he is at Oxford now — and he would not know me from Adam only he is a neighbour and used to baby-sit with me once. This is humiliating and I don't tell people.

Carson is known to do a number of strange things and walking on one leg may be one of them for all I know so I do not remark on it.

"Hello, Carson," I said, very coolly. I was past sounding warm, anyway. "Where are you going?"

Carson sits down on a stacking chair at the foot of my ladder.

"I'm going to get changed," he says.

"Did you lose your match?" I say, tactfully like Mr Evans. (I am surprised because he is next most likely after Collier to be in the final.)

"No, I won," says Carson. "But it was a Pyrrhic victory," and he starts whanging the net post with his tennis racquet, *boing boing*. (This is not good for it either, I should think.)

I have heard about Pyrrhic victories but I do not know what they are.

"What's a Pyrrhic victory?" I said.

"One you can do without," said Carson. "Named after King Pyrrhus of Epirus who remarked, after beating the Romans in a battle, 'One more win like this and we've had it', on account of the Romans badly chewing up his army."

"Oh," I said. "And did he get another win?"

"Yes," said Carson. "But then he got done over at

3

the battle of Beneventum by Curius Dentatus the famous Roman general with funny teeth. Now I just knocked spots off Pete Baldwin in the quarter-final and I'm running up to the net to thank him for a jolly good game old boy, when I turn my ankle and fall flat on my back. It's a good thing," he added, thoughtfully, "that I didn't get as far as the net, because I should have jumped over it and *then* fallen flat on my back."

I could see his point. That's the kind of thing that happens to me.

"I should have met Mick Collier in the semi-final," said Carson. "Now he'll have a walk-over. Which should suit him. He doesn't care where he puts his feet."

"Who will he play in the final?" I say, terribly pleased for Collier as well as being sorry for Carson whose ankle is definitely swelling as even I can see without my glasses which I do not wear in between matches although everyone can see I wear them because of the red mark across my nose.

"Mills or McGarrity," says Carson. "Mills is currently beating McGarrity and then Collier will beat Mills – to pulp – and no one will be surprised. I don't know why we bother," he says, tiredly, "It was a foregone conclusion." And he limps away, dragging his injured foot and not even trying to be funny about it because obviously it hurts like hell.

Then it started to rain.

Everybody came and sheltered in the canteen and griped, especially Mills and McGarrity, especially Mills who was within an inch of winning and wanted to get that over and have a crack at Collier who was a more worthy opponent. McGarrity heard all this and looked as if he would like to give Mills a dead leg – or possibly a dead head.

4

Then it stops raining and Mr Evans the games master and Miss Sylvia Truman who is our lady games master go out and skid about on the grass courts to see if they are safe. They are not. Even then I do not realize what is going to happen because Collier comes over to the dark corner where I am skulking with my cold spotty arms and starts talking to *me*!

"Jane Turner, isn't it?" he says. He must have asked somebody because he couldn't possibly know otherwise. I was only a fourth year then.

And I say, Yes.

And he says, "I see you every day on the bus, don't I?"

And I say Yes although I travel downstairs and he travels up, among the smokers although of course he doesn't smoke himself because of his athlete's lungs.

And he says, "You're an umpire today, aren't you?"

And I say Yes.

And he says, "Do you play?"

And I say Yes which I do and not badly but I don't go in for tournaments because people watch and if I was being watched I would foul it up.

"We have a court at home," he says which I know because he is a near neighbour like Carson although me and Carson live on the Glebelands Estate and the Colliers live in the Old Rectory. And then he says, *"You ought to come over and play, sometime."*

And I can't believe this but I say Yes. Yes please. Yes, I'd like that. And I still don't believe it.

And he says, "Bring your cousin and make up a foursome. That was your cousin who was sitting next to you, wasn't it, on the bus?" and I know he must have been asking about me because my cousin Dawn is only staying with us for a week.

And I say Yes, and he says, "Come on Friday, then," and I say Yes. Again. And I wonder how I can last out till Friday evening. It is only three-fifteen on Wednesday.

And then Mr Evans and Miss Sylvia Truman come in from skidding about and Mr Evans, finalist in the All-England Anthropoid Ape Championships says, "The grass is kaput. We'll have to finish up on Centre Court. Come on Collier. Come on Mills," and McGarrity says, "Mills hasn't beaten me yet, Sir," and Sir says, "Oh, well," and doesn't say, "It's a foregone conclusion," and Miss Sylvia Truman says, "Well hurry up and finish him off, Mills," in a voice that McGarrity isn't supposed to hear but does.

(If Miss Sylvia Truman *was* a man instead of just looking like one, McGarrity would take her apart, but doesn't, because she isn't. Also, she is much bigger than McGarrity.)

And Sir says, "Where's the umpire?" and I say I am and Sir says, "Can you manage?" and I say, "I haven't made any mistakes yet."

"But it's the *final*," says Fiery Fred Truman who thinks I am an imbecile – I have heard her – but I say I can manage and I am desperate to do it because of Collier playing and perhaps Sir has been fortifying himself with the flat bottle he thinks we don't know about but which we can see the outline of in his hip pocket, because he says, "All right, Jane," and I can't believe it.

But anyway, we all go out to the damp green canyon that is Centre Court and I go up my ladder and Mills finishes off McGarrity love-love-love-love and still I don't make any mistakes.

And then suddenly *everybody* is there to watch because it is Mills versus Collier and we all want Collier to win.

6

Collier comes and takes off his sweater and hangs it on the rung of my chair and says, "Don't be too hard on me, Jane," with that smile that would make you love him even if you didn't like him, and I say, "I've got to be impartial," and he smiles and I wish that I didn't have to be impartial and I am afraid that I won't be impartial.

He says, "I won't hold it against you, Jane." And he says, "Don't forget Friday."

I say, "I won't forget Friday," as loudly as I can so that as many people as possible will hear, which they do.

You can see them being surprised all round the court.

"And don't forget your cousin," he says, and I say, "Oh, she's going home on Thursday morning."

"Some other time, then," he says.

"No, no," I said. "*I* can come on Friday," but he was already walking onto the court and he just looked over his shoulder and said, "No, it doesn't matter," and all round the court you could see people not being surprised. And I was there on that lousy stinking bloody ladder and *everybody* could see me.

I thought I was going to cry and spent a long time putting my glasses on. Collier and Mills began to knock up and I got out the pencil and the score cards and broke the point off the pencil. I didn't have another one and I didn't want to show my face asking anybody to lend me one so I had to bite the wood away from the lead and of course it didn't have a proper point and made two lines instead of one. And gritty.

And then I remembered that I had to start them off so I said "Play, please. Collier to serve." He had won the toss. Naturally.

My voice had gone woolly and my glasses had

steamed over and I was sure people were laughing, even if they weren't. Then I heard this voice down by my feet saying, "Let him get on with it. If he won't play with you on Friday he can play with himself," which kind of remark would normally make me go red only I was red already. I looked down and there was Carson looking not at all well because of his foot, probably, but he gave me an evil wink and I remembered that he was a very kind person, really. I remembered that he sometimes gave me a glass of beer when he was baby-sitting. (I was only eleven, then, when he baby-sat. My mother was fussy about leaving us and there was my baby brother as well. He wasn't really sitting with *me*.)

So I smiled and he said "Watch the court, for God's sake, they've started," and they had.

"That's a point to Collier," he said, and I marked it down and dared not take my eyes off court after that, even to thank him. I looked down again when they changed ends and Carson had gone. (I asked him later where he had gone to and he said he went to throw up. I hope all this doesn't make Carson sound too *coarse*. He was in great pain. It turned out that he had broken a bone in his foot but we didn't know that, then. There are a lot of bones in the foot although you think of it as being solid — down to the toes, at any rate.)

Collier wasn't having it all his own way hooray hooray. Mills was very good too and the first set went to a tie-break. I still wasn't making any mistakes. But when they came off the court after the tie-break which Collier won, and did Wimbledonly things with towels and a bit of swigging and spitting, he kept not looking at me. I mean, you could definitely see him *not* looking at me. Everybody could see him *not* looking at me; remembering what he had said about

8

Friday and what I had said about Friday, as loudly as I could.

I was nearly crying again, and what with that and the state of the official school pencil, the score card began to be in a bit of a mess and I suddenly realized that I was putting Collier's points on the wrong line. And of course, I called out "Advantage Mills," when it should have been forty-thirty to Collier and he yelled at me to look at what I was doing.

You don't argue with the umpire. You certainly don't *yell* at the umpire, but he did. I know I was wrong but he didn't have to yell. I kept thinking about him yelling and about Friday and in the next game I made the same mistake again and he was saying "That's all I need, a cross-eyed umpire; there's eight hundred people in this school; can't we find *one* with 20-20 vision?" If Fiery Fred or Orang-Evans had been listening he might not have said it, but he was up by the net and facing away from them. He got worse and worse. Abusive.

Then Mills won the next game without any help from me and I thought, At least he's not having another walk-over, and I remembered what Carson had said. "He doesn't care where he puts his feet." And of course, after that, I couldn't help looking at his feet and Carson was right. He didn't care where he put them. He had this very fantastic service that went up about ten metres before he hit the ball, but his toes were over the base line three times out of five. I don't know why nobody noticed. I suppose they were all watching the fantastic ten metre service and anyway, nobody looks at feet.

At first I forgot that this was anything to do with me; when I did remember I couldn't bear to do anything about it, at first. Then it was Mills who was serving and I had time to think.

I thought, Why should he get away with it?

Then I thought, He gets away with everything, and I realized that Carson probably hadn't been talking about real feet but feet was all I could think of.

Collier served. His feet were not where they should have been.

"Fifteen – love."

I thought, I'll give you one more chance, because he was playing so well and I didn't want to spoil that fantastic service. But he had his chance, and he did it again. It was a beautiful shot, an ace, right down the centre line, and Mills never got near it.

I said, "Foot fault."

There was a sort of mumbling noise from everyone watching and Collier scowled but he had to play the second service. Mills tipped it back over the net and Collier never got near it.

"Fifteen all."

"Foot fault."

He was going to argue but of course he couldn't because feet is not what he looked at when he was serving.

"Fifteen – thirty." His second service wasn't very good, really.

"Foot fault."

"Fifteen – forty."

And then he did begin to look, and watching his feet he had to stop watching the ball and all sorts of things began to happen to his service.

Mills won that set.

"What the hell are you playing at, Turner?" said Collier, when they came off court and he called me a vindictive little cow while he was towelling and spitting but honestly, I never called foot fault if it wasn't.

They went back for the third set and it was

Collier's service. He glared at me like he had dead ray eyeballs and tossed up the first ball. And looked up.

And looked down at his feet.

And looked up again, but it was too late and the ball came straight down and bounced and rolled away into the crowd.

So he served again, looked up, looked down, and tried to move back and trod on his own foot and fell over.

People laughed. A laugh sounds terrible on Centre Court with all those walls to bounce off. Some of the algae had transferred itself to his shorts.

By now, *everybody* was looking at his feet.

He served a double fault.

"So who's winning?" said Alan Carson, back again and now looking greener than Collier's shorts. I knew he would understand because he *had* come back instead of going home to pass out which was what he should have been doing.

"I am," I said, miserably.

"Two Pyrrhic victories in one afternoon?" said Alan. "That must be some kind of a record."

"It must be," I said. "It's got a hole in it."

Jan Mark: "Feet is a true story insofar as I once sat in the umpire's chair at an inter-schools tennis tournament and discovered the pleasures of being impartial. Like Collier, in the story, my victim did not care where he put his feet and he had been treading on my corns all afternoon. As a writer I often find myself in the umpire's chair, looking down on the things I used to do. I rarely write about the things that I am doing now! That will happen later, when another chair becomes vacant, on another court."

THE NIGHT OUT

Robert Westall

Me and Carpet were just finishing a game of pool, working out how to pinch another game before the kids who'd booked next, when Maniac comes across.

Maniac was playing at Hell's Angels again. Home-made swastikas all over his leathers and beer-mats sewn all over his jeans. Maniac plays at everything, even biking. Don't know how we put up with him, but he hangs on. Bike Club's a tolerant lot.

"Geronimo says do you want go camping tonight?" chirps Maniac.

"Pull the other one," says Carpet. 'Cos the last we seen of Geronimo, he was pinching forks and spoons out of the Club canteen to stuff up Maniac's exhaust. So that when Maniac revved-up, he'd think his big-end had gone. Maniac always worries about his big-end; always worries about everything. Some biker.

I'd better explain all these nicknames, before you think I'm potty. Geronimo's name is really Weston; which becomes Western; which becomes Indian chief; which becomes Geronimo. Carpet's real name is Matt; but he says when he was called Matt everybody trampled on him. Some chance. Carpet's a big hard kid; but he'd always help out a mate in trouble. Maniac's really called Casey equals crazy equals Maniac. Got it?

Anyway, Geronimo himself comes over laughing, having just fastened the club-secretary to his chair by the back-buckles of his leathers, and everyone's killing themselves laughing, except the secretary who hasn't noticed yet ...

"You game?" asks Geronimo.

I was game. There was nowt else going on, except ten kids doing an all-male tribal dance right in front of the main amplifier of the disco. The rest had reached the stage where the big joke was to pour somebody's pint into somebody else's crash-helmet. Besides, it was a privilege to go anywhere with Geronimo; he could pull laughs out of the air.

"Half-an-hour; Sparwick chippie," said Geronimo, and we all made tracks for home. I managed seventy up the main street, watching for fuzz having a crafty fag in shop-doorways. But there was nobody about except middle-aged guys in dirty raincoats staring in the windows of telly-shops. What's middle age a punishment for? Is there no cure?

At home, I went straight to my room and got my tent and sleeping-bag. Don't know why I bothered. As far as Geronimo was concerned, a tent was just for letting down the guy-ropes of, on wet nights. And a sleeping-bag was for jumping on, once somebody got into it. I raided the larder and found the usual baked beans and hot-dogs. My parents didn't eat either. They bought them for me camping, on condition that I didn't nick tomorrow's lunch.

Stuck me head in the lounge. Dad had his head stuck in the telly, worrying about the plight of the Vietnamese boat-refugees. Some treat, after a hard week's work!

"Going camping. Seeya in morning."

"Don't forget your key. I'm not getting up for you in the middle of the night if it starts raining."

Which really meant I love you and take care not to break your silly neck 'cos I know what you're going

13

to get up to. But he'd never say it, 'cos I've got him well trained. Me mum made a worried kind of grab at the air, so I slammed down the visor of me helmet and went, yelling "Seeya in morning" again to drown her protests before she made them.

Moon was up, all the way to Sparwick chippie. Making the trees all silver down one side. Felt great, 'cos we were *going* somewhere. Didn't know where, but *somewhere*. Astronaut to Saturn, with Carpet and Geronimo ... and Maniac? Well, nobody expected life to be perfect ...

Carpet was there already. "What you got?" he said, slapping my top-box.

"Beans an' hotdogs. What you got?"

"Hotdogs an' beans."

"Crap!"

"Even that would make a change."

"No it wouldn't. We have that all week at the works canteen."

We sat side by side, revving-up, watching the old grannies in their curlers and carpet-slippers coming out of the chippie clutching their hot greasy packets to their boobs like they were babies, and yakking on about who's got cancer now.

"If I reach fifty, I'm goin' to commit suicide," said Carpet.

"Forty'll do me."

"Way you ride, you won't reach twenty."

Maniac rode up, sounding like a trade-in sewing-machine. He immediately got off and started revving his bike, with his helmet shoved against his rear forks.

"What's up?"

"Funny noise."

"No funnier than usual," said Carpet. But he took his helmet off and got Maniac to rev her again, and immediately spotted it was the tins in Maniac's top-box that were making the rattling. "Bad case of Heinz," he muttered to me, but he said to Maniac, "Sounds like piston-slap. We'd better get the cylinder-head off ..."

Maniac turned as white as a sheet in the light from the chippie, but he started getting his toolkit out, 'cos he knew Carpet knew bikes.

Just as well Geronimo turned up then. Carpet's crazy; he'd sooner strip a bike than a bird ...

"Where to then?" said Geronimo.

Nobody had a clue. Everybody had the same old ideas and got howled down. It's like that sometimes. We get stuck for a place to go. Then Maniac and Carpet started arguing about Jap bikes versus British, and you can't sink lower than that. In a minute they'd start eating their beans straight from the tins, tipping them up like cans of lager. Once the grub was gone, there'd be no point to going anywhere, and I'd be home before midnight and Dad would say was it morning already how time flies and all that middle-aged smartycrap.

And Geronimo had lost interest in us and was watching the cars going past down the main road. If something interesting came past worth burning off, like a Lamborghini or even a Jag XJ 12, we wouldn't see him again for the rest of the night.

So I said I knew where there was a haunted abbey. I felt a bit of a rat, 'cos that abbey was a big thing with Dad. He was a mate of the guy who owned it and he'd taken me all over it and it was a fascinating place and God knew what Geronimo would do to it ... but we'd got to go somewhere.

"What's it haunted by?" Geronimo put his helmet against mine, so his voice boomed. But he was interested.

"A nun. There was a kid riding past one night, and

this tart all clad in white steps out right under his front wheel and he claps his anchors on but he goes straight into her and arse over tip. Ruins his enamel. But when he went back there was nothing there."

"Bollocks," said Geronimo. "But I'll go for the sex-interest. What's a nun doing in an *abbey*?" He was no fool, Geronimo. He could tell a Carmelite from a camshaft when he had to.

"Ride along," he said, and took off with me on his shoulder, which is great, like fighter-pilots in the war. And I watched the street-lights sliding curved across his black helmet, and the way he changed gear smart as a whip. He got his acceleration with a long hard burst in second.

I found them the abbey gate and opened it and left it for Maniac to close. "Quiet — there's people living here."

"Throttle-down," said Geronimo.

But Maniac started going on about the abbey being private property and trespass; a real hero.

"Have a good trip home," said Geronimo. "Please drive carefully."

Maniac flinched like Geronimo'd hit him. Then mumbled "O.K. Hang on a minute, then."

Everybody groaned. Maniac was a big drinker, you see. Shandy-bitter. Lemonade. He'd never breathalyse in a million years. But it made him burp all the time, like a clapped-out Norton Commando. And he was always having to stop and go behind hedges. Only he was scared to stop, in case we shot off without him. That time, we let him get started, and *went*. Laughing so we could hardly ride, 'cos he'd be pissing all over his bulled-up boots in a panic.

It was a hell of a ride, 'cos the guy who owned the abbey kept his drive all rutted, to discourage people like us. Geronimo went up on his foot-rests like a jockey, back straight as a ruler. Nobody could ride like Geronimo; even my Dad said he rode like an Apache.

It was like scrambling; just Geronimo's straight back and the tunnel of trees ahead, white in the light of Geronimo's quartz-halogen, and the shining red eyes of rabbits and foxes staring out at us, then shooting off. And our three engines so quiet, and Maniac far behind, revving up like mad, trying to catch up. I wished it could go on forever till a sheet of water shot up inside my leathers so cold I forgot if I was male or female ...

Geronimo had found a rut full of water, and soaked me beautifully. He was staring back at me, laughing through his visor. And here was another rut coming up. Oh, hell — it was lucky I always cleaned my bike on Saturday mornings. Anyway, he soaked me five times, but I soaked him once, and I got Carpet twice. And Maniac caught up; and then fell off when Carpet got *him*. And then we were at the abbey.

A great stretch of moonlit grass, sweeping down to the river. And the part the monks used to live in, which was now a stately home, away on the right all massive and black, except where our lights shone on hundreds and hundreds of windows. And the part that used to be the abbey church was on the left. Henry the Eighth made them pull that all down, so there was nothing left but low walls, and the bases of columns sticking out of the turf about as high as park benches, like black rotten teeth. And at the far end of that was a tall stone cross.

"That's the Nun's Grave," I said. "But it's not really. Just some old bits and pieces of the abbey that they found in the eighteenth century and put together to make a good story ..."

"Big 'ead," said Geronimo. "Let's have a look." He climbed onto the base of the first column; and, waving his arms about, leapt for the base of the second column. Screaming like a banshee. "I AAAAAMM the Flying Nun." It was a fantastic leap; about twelve feet. He made it, though his boots scrawped heavily on the sandstone blocks. I shuddered, and looked towards the house. Luckily, there wasn't a light showing. Country people went to bed early. I hoped.

"I AAAAAAAAMMM the Flying Nun," wailed Geronimo, "and I'm in LOOOOOOVE with the Flying Abbot. But I'm cheating on him with the Flying Doctor."

He attempted another death-defying leap, missed his footing, and nearly ruined his married future.

"Amendment," said Carpet. "He *was* the Flying Nun."

"Never fear. The Flying Nun will fly again," croaked Geronimo from the grass. His helmet appeared to have turned back-to-front, and he was holding his crotch painfully.

"Amendment," said Carpet. "The Flying Soprano will fly again."

We were all so busy falling about (even Maniac had stopped worrying about trespass) that we didn't see the bloke at first. But there he was, standing in the shadow of his great house, screaming like a nut-case.

"Hooligans! Vandals!" Sounded like he was having a real fit.

"Is that that mate of yours?" Carpet asked me.

"Mate of my Dad's," I said.

"Your Dad knows some funny people. Is he an out-patient, or has he climbed over the wall?" Carpet turned to the distant raging figure and amiably pointed the two fingers of scorn.

He shouldn't have done that. Next second, a huge four-legged shape came tearing towards us over the grass. Doing a ton with its jaws wide open and its rotten great fangs shining in the moonlight. It didn't make a sound; not like any ordinary dog. And the little figure by the house was shouting things like, "Kill, kill, kill!" He didn't seem at all like the guy I met when Dad took me round the house ...

Maniac turned and scarpered. Geronimo was still lying on the grass trying to get his helmet straight. And the rotten great dog was making straight at him. I couldn't move.

But Carpet did. He ran and straddled over Geronimo. Braced himself, and he was a big lad; there was eighty kilos of him.

The dog leapt, like they do in the movies. Carpet thrust his gauntletted fist right up its throat. Carpet rocked, but he didn't fall. The dog was chewing on his glove like mad, studs and all.

"Naughty doggy," said Carpet reprovingly, and gave it a terrific clout over the ear with his other hand.

Two more clouts and the dog stopped chewing. Three, and let it go. Then Carpet kicked it in the ribs. Sounded like the big bass drum.

"Heel, Fido!" said Carpet.

The dog went for Geronimo, who was staggering to his feet; and got Carpet's boot again. It fell back, whimpering.

The next second, a tiny figure was flailing at Carpet. "Leave my dog *alone*. How *dare* you hit my dog. I'll have the RSPCA on you — that's all you hooligans are good for, mistreating dogs." He was literally foaming at the mouth. "I don't know what this country's coming to ..."

"It's going to the dogs," said Carpet. He pushed the man gently away with one great hand, and held him at arm's length. "Look, mate," he said sadly, wagging one finger of a well-chewed gauntlet, "take the Hound of the Baskervilles home. It's time for his Meaty Chunks ..."

"I am going," spluttered the little guy, "to call the police."

"I would, mate," said Carpet. "There's a highly-dangerous dog loose round here somewhere ..."

The pair of them slunk off. Maniac returned from the nearest bushes, to the sound of cheers. Geronimo slapped Carpet on the shoulder and said "Thanks, mate," in a voice that had me green with envy. And we all buggered off. After we had ridden three times round the house for luck. Including the steps in the formal garden.

"There's another way out," I said, "at the far end."

The far drive seemed to go on forever. Or was it that we were riding slowly, because Carpet was having trouble changing gear with his right hand. I think the dog had hurt him right through the glove; but that was not something Carpet would ever admit.

Just before we went out through the great gates, with stone eagles on their gateposts, we passed a white Hillman Imp, parked on the right well off the road, under the big horse-chestnut trees of the avenue. It seemed empty as we passed, though, oddly enough, it had its sunshields down, which was a funny thing to happen at midnight.

Outside, Geronimo held up his right hand, US Cavalry-fashion, and we all stopped.

"Back," said Geronimo. "Lights out. Throttle down. Quiet."

"What?"

But he was gone back inside. All we could do was follow. It was lucky the moon was out when he stopped. Or we'd all have driven over him and flattened him.

"*What?*" we all said again.

But he just said, "Push your bikes."

We all pushed our bikes, swearing at him.

"Quiet!"

The white Hillman glimmered up in the moonlight.

"Thought so," said Geronimo. A white arm appeared for a moment, behind the steering wheel and vanished again.

Maniac sniggered.

"You can't *do* it," said Carpet. "Not in a Hillman Imp!"

"You have a wide experience of Hillman Imps?" asked Geronimo.

"Let's stay and watch," said Maniac.

Carpet and I looked at Geronimo uneasily.

"What do you think *I* am?" said Geronimo, crushing Maniac like he was a beetle. "Mount up, lads. Right. Lights, sound, music, enter the villain."

Four headlamps, three of them quartz-halogen, coned in on the Imp. I noticed it was L-reg. It shone like day, but for a long moment nothing else happened.

Then a head appeared; a bald head, with beady eyes and a rat-trap mouth. Followed by a naked chest, hairy as a chimpanzee. The eyes glared; a large fist was raised and shaken.

"Switch off," said Geronimo. "And *quiet*."

We sat and listened. There was the mother and father of a row going on inside the Imp.

"Drive me *home*!"

"It was nothing. Just a car passing. They've gone now."

We waited; the voices got lower and lower. Silence.

"Start your engines," said Geronimo. "*Quietly*."

"What for?" asked Maniac plaintively.

"You'll see," said Geronimo, and laughed with pure delight.

He and Carpet and me had electric starter-motors; which of course started up quietly, first press of the button. Good old Jap-crap. Maniac, buying British and best, had to kick his over and over again.

"I'm going to buy you a new flint for that thing," said Carpet.

Maniac's bike started at last.

"Lights," said Geronimo.

There was a wild scream; then an even wilder burst of swearing. The bald head reappeared. The car-lights came on; its engine started and revved.

"*Move*!" shouted Geronimo, curving his bike away between the tree-trunks.

"Why?" yelled Maniac.

"He'll never live to see twenty," said Carpet, as we turned together through the branches, neat as a pair of performing dolphins.

Then the Imp was after us, screeching and roaring in second gear fit to blow a gasket.

We went out of those gates like Agostini, down through the slumbering hamlet of Blackdore and up towards the moors. We were all riding four-hundreds, and we could have lost the Imp in ten seconds. But it was more fun to dawdle at seventy, watching the Imp trying to catch up. God, it was cornering like a lunatic, right over on the wrong side of the road. Another out-patient got over the wall. Even more than most motorists, that is.

And old Maniac was not keeping up. That bloody British bike of his; that clapped-out old Tiger was missing on one rotten cylinder.

He was lagging further and further behind. The

Imp's lights seemed to be drawing alongside his. He was riding badly, cowering against the hedge, not leaving himself enough room to get a good line into his corners. I knew how he'd be feeling; mouth dry as brickdust; knees and hands shaking almost beyond control.

Then the Imp did draw alongside, and made a tremendous side-swipe at him, trying to knock him off into the hedge at seventy. The guy in the Imp was trying to kill Maniac. And there was nothing we could do. I pulled alongside Carpet and pointed behind. But Carpet had seen already and didn't know what to do either.

Then Geronimo noticed. Throttled back, waved us through. In my rear-view mirror I watched him drop further and further back, until he seemed just in front of the Imp's bumper. Up went two fingers. Again and again. He put his thumb to his nose and waggled his fingers. I swear he did — I saw them in silhouette against the Imp's lights; though afterwards Carpet made out I couldn't have done and that it was something I made up.

At last, the Imp took notice; forgot Maniac cowering and limping beside the hedge, and came after Geronimo.

"Out to the left," gestured Carpet, and we shot off down a side-road, turned and came back behind the lunatic's car.

So we saw it all in comfort. Oh; Geronimo could have walked away from him; Geronimo could do a hundred and ten if he liked. But just as he was going to, he saw this riding-school in a field on the left, on the outskirts of the next village, Chelbury. You know the kind of place — all white-painted oildrums and red-and-white striped poles where little female toffs try to learn to show-jump.

In went Geronimo. Round and round went Geronimo. Round the barrels, under the poles. And round and round went the Imp. Into the barrels and smashing the poles to smithereens. He couldn't drive for toffee — like a mad bull in a china-shop and Geronimo the bull-fighter. *Boing, boing, boing* went the drums. Splinter, splinter, splinter in the moonlight went the poles.

Geronimo could have gone on forever. But lights were coming on in the houses; curtains being pulled back on the finest display of trick-riding the villagers of Chelbury will ever see — not that they'd have the sense to appreciate it.

Just as Maniac turned up, minus a bit of paint, we heard the siren of the cop-car. Some toffee-nosed gent had been on the phone.

Of course the cop-car, bumping across the grass through the shambles, made straight for Geronimo; the fuzz always blame the motorcyclist and the Imp had stopped its murder-attempts by that time.

"You young lunatic," said the fuzz getting out, "You've caused damage worth thousands ..."

Geronimo gestured at his bike, which hadn't a scratch on it in the cop-car's headlights. Then he nodded at the Imp, which had four feet of striped pole stuck inside its front bumper.

Then the fuzz noticed that the guy at the wheel was completely starkers. And that there was a long-haired blonde on the back seat trying to put her jumper on inside-out and back-to-front. The fuzz kept losing his grip on the situation every time the blonde wriggled. Well, they're human too. All very enjoyable ...

We got back to Carpet's place about seven, still laughing so much we were wobbling all over the road. We always end up at Carpet's place after a night out.

It's a nice little detached bungalow on top of a hill. And we always weave round and round Carpet's Dad's crazy-paving, revving like mad. And Carpet's Mum always throws open the one upstairs window and leans out in the blue dressing-gown, and asks what the hell we want. And Geronimo always asks, innocent-like, "This is the motorway cafe, isn't it?" And Carpet's Mum always calls him a cheeky young tyke, and comes down and lets us in and gives us cans of lager and meat pies while she does a great big fry-up for breakfast. And we lie about till lunchtime with our boots on the furniture, giving her cheek, and she's loving it and laughing. I used to wonder why she put up with us, till I realized she was just that glad to have Carpet back alive.

And that was our night out.

On Monday night, when I got home from work, Dad took me in the front room alone. I knew something was up. Had the guy from the abbey rumbled us? But Dad gave me a whisky, and I knew it was worse.

He told me Geronimo was dead; killed on his bike. I wouldn't believe it. No bastard motorist could ever get Geronimo.

Then he told me how it happened. On a bend, with two-metre stone walls either side. Geronimo was coming home from work in the dark. He'd have been tired. He was only doing fifty; on his right side, one metre out from the kerb. The police could tell from the skid-marks.

The car was only a lousy Morris Marina. Overtaking on a blind corner. The driver didn't stop; but the other driver got his number. When the police breathalysed him, he was pissed to the eyeballs.

I believed it then; and I cried.

We gave him a real biker's funeral. A hundred and seventy bikes followed him through town, at fifteen kilometres an hour, two by two. I've never seen such disciplined riding. Nobody fell off; though a few of the lads burned their clutches out. We really pinned this town's ears back. They know what bikers are now; bikers are *together*.

The Pope died about that time. The Pope only had twelve motorbike outriders; Geronimo had a hundred and seventy. If he met the Pope in some waiting-room or other, Geronimo would have pointed that out. But laughing, mind. He was always laughing, Geronimo.

Afterwards, we all went back to the Club and got the drinks in. Then there was a bloody horrible silence; the lads were really down, like I've never seen them. It was terrible.

Then Fred, the Club secretary gets to his feet, and points at the pool table, where Geronimo used to sit, putting the players off their stroke by wriggling his backside.

"If he was standing there," said Fred, "if he could see you now, d'you know what he'd say? He'd say 'What you being so miserable for, you stupid nerks?'" And suddenly, though nobody saw or heard anything, he *was* there, and it was all right. And everybody was falling over themselves to tell Geronimo-stories and laughing.

We all went to the court-case too, all in our gear. The Clerk to the Court tried to have us thrown out; but one or two of us have got a few O Levels, and enough sense to hire our own lawyer. Who told the Clerk to the Court where he got off. We were all British citizens, of voting age, as good as anybody else. Har-har.

And the police proved everything against the driver

of the Marina. He lost his licence, of course. Then the judge said six months imprisonment.

Then he said sentence suspended for two years ...

Why? 'Cos he was middle-aged and big and fat with an expensive overcoat and a posh lawyer? 'Cos he belonged to the same golf-club as the judge?

The lads gave a kind of growl. The Clerk was shaking so much he couldn't hold his papers. So was the Marina-driver, who'd been whispering and grinning at his lawyer till then.

The Clerk began shouting for silence; going on about contempt of court. Fred got up. He's a hundred kilos of pure muscle, and he's about forty-five with a grown-up son in the Club.

"Not contempt, your honour. More disgust, like."

I think the lads might have gone too far then. But Geronimo's Mum (she looked very like him) put her hand on Fred's arm and asked him to take her home. And when Fred went we all followed; though a few fingers went up in the air behind backs.

Maniac and Carpet and me tried going on riding together. But it didn't work out. Whenever we rode together, there was a sort of terrible hole formed, where Geronimo should be. Maniac went off and joined the Merchant Navy, 'cos he couldn't stand this town any more. He still sends Carpet and me postcards from Bahaein and Abu Dhabi (clean ones too!). And we put them on the mantelpiece and forget them.

Carpet and I went on riding; even bought bigger bikes. I still see him sometimes, but we never stop for more than two minutes' chat.

But when I ride alone, that's different. You see you can't hear very much inside your helmet, when your engine's running. And the helmet cuts down your view to the side as well. So when we need to talk to each other on the move, we have to pull alongside and yell and yell. And when you first notice a guy doing that, it oftens comes over funny. Well, I keep thinking I hear him; that he's just lurking out of the corner of my eye. I just know he's somewhere about; you *can't* kill someone like Geronimo.

I got engaged last week. Jane's a good lass, but she made one condition. That I sell my bike and buy a car. She says she wants me to live to be a grandfather. And when my Mum heard her say it, she suddenly looked ten years younger.

So I'm taking this last ride to the abbey in the moonlight, and I've just passed Sparwick chippie. And the moon is making one side of the trees silver, and I'm *going* somewhere. Only I'm not going with Geronimo; I'm getting further away from Geronimo all the time. Nearer to the old grannies with their hair in curlers coming out of the chippie clutching their hot greasy bundles. The middle-aged guys staring in the telly-shop windows.

And I'm not sure I like it.

Robert Westall: "Motorcyclists fascinate me. I'm very proud to be President of the Cheshire Albion Motorcycle Club. They're very generous with their technical chat — I couldn't have written the story without them. Myself, I never got beyond a Honda 50. I admire motorcyclists like hell, but I'm never sorry to hear when one has taken to four wheels; they're among the best people we have; too good to die young."

HOMEWORK

Mary Sullivan

"Why should *I* go?" said Stephen, "I'm not his
nursemaid. Why can't he get home from school by
himself? Who ever came to fetch me?" He picked
the last bit of mud out of the ridges of his climbing
boots, and put them on the floor.

"I did. For about fifty years," said his mother.
"Those things will crack if you leave them near the
radiator. Get them up to your own room, out of the
way. And here's the shopping list, and hurry up,
Tim'll cry if he's left till last."

"Little booby," muttered Stephen, crashing
upstairs with the boots. He went out, came back for
the list and the shopping bag, and set off again. He
bought an evening paper and stood in the street for a
long time, combing the motorbike columns in the
small ads, and reading about Sharkey being transferred for a quarter of a million.

When he got to the school he found Tim sitting in
the playground with his shoe-laces undone, crying.

"Look," said Stephen. "You go like this and like
this and like that, and there's a bow. How many more
times? Now, where's your coat?"

"Don't know," said Tim, "Didn't have one."

"You must have done," said Stephen, "It was
raining this morning. Come and look for it. Oh, *come
on*!" he shouted, as Tim put his dirty hands over his
dirty face.

Stephen went into the little kids' cloakroom, where

the rows of hooks and small washbasins seemed about level with his knees. Tim's coat was on the floor, under some shoe-lockers.

"Put it on, Tim," said Stephen, "I don't want to carry it, and you'll lose it otherwise."

"I'm hot," said Tim.

"*On*, I said." Stephen pulled the little boy roughly towards and did up the buttons. Tim walked behind him towards the shops, stopping when Stephen stopped and refusing to take his hand.

"I know what," said Stephen, "Let's go and see the diggings."

Tim stood on one foot so as to scratch the back of his knee with the other, and then, beginning to smile, he caught up with Stephen and they went along together.

When their mother was a child there had been houses on the corner of Tyler Street. Then it was a bomb-site; then a car park, and now a supermarket was being built there. The deep excavations were fenced and boarded off, but inspection holes had obligingly been left at different heights all the way round, so that passers-by could watch.

"What are those arches?" said Tim, "Those pink ones?"

"Where?" Stephen bent down to look through, where Tim was looking. On the left side of the large oblong site a wide trench had been dug, twenty feet deeper than the level surface now marked out for the supermarket foundations. Along the side marched rosy brick arches. Dark earth was packed into the spaces between their columns, but their outer surfaces were as sharp and clean as if the bricklayers had finished work that afternoon.

"I don't know," said Stephen. "It looks like the foundations of something quite big, only those bricks look so new."

There was no one working, and even the watchman's hut was empty.

"It's their tea-time," said Stephen. They did the shopping along Tyler Street, and went home.

"Fish pie, disgusting," said Stephen to his mother as he sat down. "You know I hate it, what d'you go on making it for?"

"There's others live here besides you," she answered. "Timmy likes it, so do I, and your dad. He'll be in soon, so I'd go up and get some of that homework done if I were you, after last night."

"What about last night?" mumbled Stephen. His mother sliced the bread in silence.

"Just because I forgot Gran was coming," said Stephen angrily.

"Remembered, more like," said his mother, "and stayed out till she'd gone, and went to bed without doing any work at all."

"I was tired," said Stephen, taking the tomato sauce and entirely covering his fish pie.

"Those exams are in ten days," said his mother. "I don't see Jessica hanging round here, or Sandy, or that Billings boy. They're getting on with their work; they haven't got time for larking about."

"Jessica used to," said Stephen scornfully, "She's suddenly got this fixation about going to art school."

"Yes, well," said his mother.

Later on Stephen went up to his room to work, but he took his radio with him, and the April issue of *Climbing*. He used paper of different colours to make lists of the revision he had to do, and timetables of when he was going to do it, but after that he settled down to a long article on experimental climbing equipment, and an interview with Joe Brown. He read for an hour. He heard his father come in, and the television go on. It might be unwise to appear for a while.

He lay on his bed among a jumble of folders and notebooks, looking at the charcoal drawing of his own face that Jessica had done once. The mouth was wrong, and the hair had been suggested with a smudging technique which hadn't worked very well, but in the eyes and brow he thought he recognized himself.

He got up suddenly and went down to the kitchen. He took a banana from the bowl and opened the back door.

"Stephen!" called his father, "Don't go out till you've done that homework!"

"I'm doing it, dad," answered Stephen, "I'm just going round to ask Jessica something."

"Be back by —" Stephen shut the door. He got out his bike and rode round to Jessica's.

"Hello, Steve," she said. "Come in a minute. Come through, I'm working in the kitchen. Look at these."

Spread on the table were a dozen photos of the pink brick arches.

"I saw them this afternoon, with Tim," said Stephen, looking at the pictures closely. "What are they, Jess?"

"Foundations of Tyler's Brewery," said Jessica, "Eighteenth century I think. Pulled down about 1860 to make way for houses, as far as I've discovered. All that site will get filled in again next week. I'm doing a thing about Tyler Street for the architecture part of my exams." She bent over her work again.

"Yes," said Stephen vaguely. "Jess, I came to ask you something."

"Mmmm?"

"Come climbing on Saturday? We could go to Harrison's Rocks again, and see how you get on this time."

Jessica made no reply.

"Jess?"

She looked up. "Steve, I don't like climbing all that much you know, and there's nothing else to do except hang round at the bottom admiring you. Won't Sandy go with you?"

"Oh, I expect so," said Stephen. "Haven't asked her." After a while he said "Anyway, I'll go now, as you're busy." He lingered at the front door. " 'Bye then, Jess," he called.

" 'Bye."

Stephen rode off. He turned north, away from home, and putting his head down, began to sprint along the fast road out of town.

As he approached the roundabout, he took his feet off the pedals and let the bike swoop into the bend. A Honda appeared, crowding up from nowhere, so close that Stephen was nudged into the grassy bank, and he found himself on the ground with his bike on top of him.

He struggled up. "Fool!" he screamed at the black leather back speeding away. The Honda circled the roundabout and returned. "Fool!" bellowed Stephen again. The Honda came right up to him, and the man half raised his yellow crash helmet.

"Did you say something, sonny?"

"What about this?" said Stephen. He poked out the broken bits of three spokes in his back wheel.

"Have to get a new tricycle, won't you?" said the man over his shoulder, as the Honda stormed away.

It was getting dark when Stephen pushed his bike slowly back into town. His legs were still trembling and he was sweating. He left the bike outside the Duke of York, and went into the saloon bar.

"Pint of bitter, please," he said quickly.

"Can you read?" asked the landlord, pointing to a stained notice pinned above the bar. " 'It is an offence', see, for you to buy it or me to sell it. As if you didn't know."

Stephen turned away.

"Come back when you're legal," said the landlord. "I don't know," he appealed to his regulars. "Cost me my licence. Kids these days."

Stephen trudged towards home. Lights were on everywhere now, but the building site in Tyler Street, glimpsed through the inspection holes, was a shadowy pit. He leaned his bike against the boards, and stared down.

Some of his climbing stuff was still in his saddle-bag. He took from it a knife, a torch, and a coil of rope which he slipped over his head and across his shoulder. He stood on the saddle of his bike and found that he could reach the projections of a metal sign on the other side of the boards. He pulled himself up, and slithered rapidly over and down.

It took a long time to pick his way to the wide trench, among crates and piles of rubbish. He kicked an empty oil drum and stood in fright listening to the clang. He went on. A tractor with a trailer had been left a few yards from the edge of the trench. Stephen took off his rope and tied it to the tow-bar. He ran the rope to the trench, threw it in and let himself down.

There had been some work here since he and Tim passed by. The brick arches were no longer perfect: someone had been at them with a pick axe, and his torch showed lumps and crumbs of the brickwork scattered on the ground. Stephen tried a corner brick with the point of his knife, but it was firm. He scratched and tapped at others, ran his fingers along further, and found a brick-shaped hole. He flicked light round the trench. The complete brick was lying at a distance, flung there. He picked it up. It was lighter than he expected, with coarse pores and an uneven surface. He zipped it into his jacket and shinned up the rope.

A moment later, hanging from the sign above the fence, he felt down with his feet for the bike.

"Oh, it's you, is it?" said the watchman, leaning on Stephen's bike yards away. "Would you be wanting this?"

Stephen let go and dropped. "Oh Christ, my elbow!"

"Your elbow my foot. What have you been thieving?"

"Nothing." Stephen held his arm. "A brick, one brick, that had been dug out already. Look."

The watchman came over and made Stephen take off his jacket. "What did you want to do a stupid thing like that for?"

"Fun."

The watchman grunted. "Here, then," he said, pushing Stephen's bike towards him. "Now clear off, and don't let me catch you in there again."

"Having trouble, Ken?" A policeman stuck his head out from the car which had drawn up by the watchman's hut. Stephen stood very still.

"No, thanks," said the watchman, "Just having a bit of a chat here."

"Right. 'Night," said the policeman.

Stephen took his bike. "Thanks."

"Cheers," said the watchman.

Stephen wheeled his bike round to Jessica's. He took out a map of Kent from his saddle bag, and tore off the front cover. On the back he wrote: "This brick came from the foundations of Tyler's Brewery in Tyler Street, and is about 200 years old. Presented to Jessica Hare by Stephen Linton." He put the brick on Jessica's doorstep, tucked his message under it, and went away.

"Is that you, Stephen?" his father called. "You can come and watch the wrestling if you've done your work."

Wrestling. Two fat blokes pretending to fight, while his father shouted "Go on, give it to him!" and knocked his cup over.

Stephen went in. "Finished it."

"What was it, anyway?" said his father suspiciously.

"A bit of history project. And some social sciences," said Stephen.

"What's that, when it's at home?" said his father, without taking his eyes off the screen.

"Oh, politics. Psychology. Human relations. That kind of thing," said Stephen, throwing the cat off his armchair. "Can I have some of that tea?"

Mary Sullivan: "In Holborn in central London, near where I live, there's a 7-acre children's playground where adults are admitted only if they have children with them. Some recent building work revealed the perfectly-preserved foundations of the 18th century orphanage which used to stand there. Eventually they were filled in and covered by a new football pitch, but not before my husband had climbed down and taken the 250-year-old, dark pink brick which gave me the idea for Homework."

A MOTHER'S FONDNESS

Marion Rachel Stewart

The Mother

I began to worry and fidget by half past five. Two
buses had gone by and she had not come home from
school. I thought of all the places she could go to and
became afraid because there were so many. My
husband was working in Glasgow and my father, who
stayed with us, was on holiday. The house was empty.
I was afraid. Not of being alone but she would have
phoned to tell me if she was going away anywhere.
My stomach turned, I felt hungry but could not eat,
tired but could not sleep, tormented by my
imagination.

At six o'clock I phoned her friend but she had no
idea where she was and suggested I phone several
people who were other schoolfriends. I phoned them
all but no one knew and said they would phone back
if they found out where she was. I took the car into
town. There was a girl she was friendly with who lived
in a house on the way to town. She hadn't a phone so
I went to the door.

"Elaine, have you seen Cathie?" It was hard to
speak as the cries of pain echoed through my head. I
was too embarrassed to stay, I had started to cry and
my eyes were red and sore. I went into all the cafés
she talked of. It was no use. I went home and found
myself waiting for the phone to ring. It did several
times. Always someone to ask if I had found her. At
nine o'clock I answered the phone for the millionth

time. It was Mrs Wilson, Elaine's mother. She said Cathie was at their house. I felt as though the greatest load had been lifted from my heart. Again I took the car and drove into town. She was very quiet and looked at me coldly. She thanked Elaine and got into the car. We said nothing but I wanted to be angry, I wanted to show how worried I had been. I knew that she would not see my anger as love for her. It seemed as though she hated me and wanted to hurt me, but I could tell as she sat stiffly and unmoved that she had no idea this was possible. I was as pleasant as I could be and she answered all the countless questions in a calm indifferent manner. I had failed. I could not get through to her. She could not see the agony I had gone through because of her. It was my fault she was as she was. I had brought myself pain.

When we got home we watched television and it seemed as though nothing had happened at all. It was forgotten, pushed away out of sight. That night I prayed it would never happen again.

The Daughter

After school I met Caroline and as she had borrowed some records of mine I decided to go round to her house and collect them. I didn't really know her all that well but she was very easy to get on with. She didn't go to the same places as I did but occasionally invited me to her house and things like that. I didn't usually go, simply because I couldn't be bothered. I hardly even saw her because we were at different schools but when we met we had a good long chat and told each other all our news.

I didn't feel like going home anyway – perhaps it was because I was getting annoyed with my mother – well, not annoyed but it had become too tense being with her. We couldn't have a conversation without it becoming a row. I think she resented me a bit. I don't know why. It made things easier when I went out; I didn't have to face up to her. She really annoyed me sometimes because any row was forgotten too quickly, as though it was a routine, as though she wasn't bothered. Any arguments were never about anything important but she made them seem trivial immediately afterwards. She made me feel foolish and small. It was horrible, I hated it happening. I had begun to keep out of her way as much as possible.

Caroline and I had a good long talk about school and other things that worried us. We listened to records for ages in complete silence, not saying a word. I suddenly realised I had missed both buses and would have to try and get the eight o'clock one.

Caroline decided we should go to the loch until it was time for my bus. By the time we had walked across the causeway and back I had missed it.

"Mum'll go daft," I said suddenly, beginning to worry.

"Look, she's going to be mad anyway so it doesn't matter how late you are."

That was fair reasoning but I was hungry and cold and I thought I'd like to get home.

"No, I'd better go now," I said. I left and started walking through town. I was passing Elaine's house so I went in to see her.

"Your mother's going daft, she's been phoning everyone. She was here, she was in town twice, she's even been to the police station." Elaine stopped and took my arm.

"Oh God," I said, "Oh no, you're joking!"

"Come in."

I sat down and buried my face in my hands. She would be furious. What was I going to say to her?

This meant another row.

"Elaine, I don't want to go home. Can't I stay here?"

"You'll have to face up to her as soon as possible. That's typical of you Cathie, you run away from everything. You'll have to face up to it."

Mrs Wilson came in. I was scared she would be angry too.

"Cathie I'm going to the phone box to phone your mother now."

My mother knocked on the door and Elaine answered. She stood quietly at the living room door.

I was angry. There had been so much fuss and now she was acting as if nothing had happened. I thanked Elaine and got into the car. I didn't see any point in talking about it so I kept very quiet and pretended I wasn't bothered. She didn't even ask where I'd been until we were halfway home.

There was no way I could show her how hurt I really was. She simply didn't care about me and I couldn't let her see how much that hurts. It was no good: she had already forgotten it – just like everything else.

Marion Rachel Stewart lives in Scotland. She wrote A Mother's Fondness *when she was fourteen, and it first appeared as an award winning entry in the sixteenth* Daily Mirror Children's Literary Competition.

THAT DOG

Freda Kelsall

"I don't want to go," Sylvia had told her mother
firmly. "I can move in with Penny or Clare for a
year. I want to stay here with my friends."

Then her mother had burst into tears, and Sylvia
had felt mean and wretched, and realized that there
was no alternative. She would be leaving London
SE9, and the warm, hugging darkness of the disco,
and the lighthearted nonsense of sunbathing in the
park with the crowd after school, and everything that
was fun and familiar.

She hadn't told Penny and Clare yet. They stood
together, not singing the Assembly hymn because
they had all decided the previous Wednesday that
they didn't believe in God. Penny and Clare would be
heartbroken.

A prefect, Philip Rowntree, was reading the Bible
passage in his stuck-up voice. He had finished his "A"
levels three weeks previously, and most of the sixth
form had vanished to hitch-hike abroad or get jobs.
But Philip was so rich, and such a drip, he wouldn't
need to leave before the end of term, or want to.

Heads were bowed for the prayers, and Sylvia's
long brown hair fell forward. She had washed it the
night before and it smelt nice. To her horror, in the
privacy of her hair, she felt she was going to cry. She
fought hard against the lump in her throat.

Penny and Clare could come for holidays in the
country.

She could make return visits, and see the old crowd, and go to the disco and the park with them. It would be all right.

The prayers were over, and Sylvia tossed back her hair. She could breathe easily, no trouble. Her eyes behind her large round spectacles were still dry. "But if the worst comes to the worst," she thought, "I'll pretend I've got hay fever."

The headmaster was giving out the announcements, mainly concerned with practice for Sports Day, and inter-house tennis, and bubble-gum stuck under chairs in the canteen. He had smiled cheerfully when Sylvia had taken him the letter from her mother.

"Moving away? I'm sorry to hear it, Sylvia, we shall miss you. But you'll take an excellent report to your new school, and I'm sure you'll do very well."

She had been disappointed. After all his advice about which examination subjects she ought to take in the coming year, she'd expected her news to land like a bombshell on his desk. But he'd waved her away with a "Come and say goodbye before you go", and returned his attention to the new first-years' timetable.

"... three-month old mongrel dog," he was saying from the platform. "Anyone able to offer a good home should see Mrs Binns after ... and I must stress this, boys and girls, *after* it has been discussed with your parents. Thank you, Mr Clark."

There was a concerted fidget as Dennis Clark struck up "March Militaire" on the piano, and the younger classes began to file out clutching satchels and comics. At this stage in the term, the teachers were easing up, and the word had gone out that non-athletes who weren't needed on the sports field should bring something to read.

Sylvia was a non-athlete. Winter was her favourite

time in school, with carol concerts and the annual Gilbert and Sullivan operetta. She was probably the only fourth-year who couldn't be relied on to catch a ball or clear a hurdle, but she had the best soprano voice in the Music Society.

"I've had you three dear girls excused from classes," declared the geography teacher as they left the hall. "Will you mend some atlases for me?"

Penny and Clare looked at each other, then at Sylvia. "All right," said Clare, "We don't mind."

Sylvia could imagine the usual comment recurring on her report: "Always a helpful member of the form" and her mother reading it and saying "I wish you were more like that at home".

Penny was the tidy, organized one of the trio. She set Clare the task of checking a pile of dog-eared atlases, sorting out the ones with loose pages in the wrong order from those with pages absolutely missing. Sylvia was given the glue and adhesive tape to play with, and Penny herself browsed through the rude doodles of idle hands, rubbing out all but the genuinely funny ones.

Sylvia told them in the quiet of the store room that she wouldn't be with them next term.

Clare did not seem to be in the least bit heartbroken. She was very interested. "Hampshire? I've been there, it's lovely countryside." Penny frowned to put her thoughts in order, then said, "I hope they're doing the same syllabus at your new school, or you won't half be in a mess. What will happen if all the set books are different?"

Sylvia's eyes filled. It was no good pretending to these two that she had hay fever. Clare put an arm round her.

"Don't be an idiot. We'll come and see you, won't we, Penny?"

Penny nodded. "We'll have to find jobs for a few weeks first," she said. "And when we've enough holiday money, we'll bring our bikes down on the train. By then you'll have discovered the best places to go to, Sylv, and you can show us round."

Clare agreed. She always agreed with Penny. Sylvia had an odd feeling that her tragic separation from them, to live in an alien place, was fitting very nicely into Penny's plans for the summer.

Sylvia swallowed. "Good idea. Quiet lanes. There's not much joy biking round here, dodging the traffic."

Penny fixed her with a hard, challenging look. "You know, you really ought to have that dog."

"What?"

"That dog. The one that's going to be put down if nobody wants it."

"I don't know anything about dogs. I don't know what you're on about."

"You must have been dreaming in Assembly, then." Penny had the long-suffering expression she wore when Sylvia was being dense. "Mrs Binns is trying to find a home for another of her RSPCA rejects. I bet all the little first-years will be bursting with enthusiasm, and all their parents will say a flat 'no'. They're right, too. London's no place for dogs. But he'd have a lovely life with you. Oh, Sylvia, you've stuck that map of Africa in upside down."

At break, the music teacher, Dennis Clark, stopped her on the stairs. "Sylvia, I've just heard you're leaving us?"

"Yes, sir."

"Well, don't let your singing go to pot, lass, you've made great strides. By the way, haven't you still got a vocal score of *Pirates* for next term? You'll not forget to let me have it back, will you?"

"No sir, I'll bring it in tomorrow."

"Good." He sighed. "I don't know who can play Mabel. Doreen Loach might manage it, but her top notes are a bit thin."

"She'll cope." Sylvia hated the idea. She wanted to be under the lights herself, in a pretty Victorian costume, with lovely-smelling greasepaint on her face and pure sounds rippling out of her, and all the applause at the end. Doreen Loach wouldn't be as good, but yes, she would cope.

"And something else," Dennis Clark said sternly. "The hymn-singing in Assembly has gone off the boil. There's a certain person not trying. Don't think that because my back is towards you I don't know." He grinned and clapped her on the shoulder. "If I miss seeing you again, all the best. You've been jolly useful. Without you and Rowntree, the Music Society will have to find new talent."

Sylvia turned away. "I'm just a mass of useful functions," she thought. "Nobody really cares about me at all." She clumped heavy-footed down the stairs, her glasses steaming up. Penny and Clare had gone on ahead to see if either of them had been picked for the fourth-year mixed relay team.

She found herself outside the school secretary's office, where Mrs Binns was on the telephone and handing out lost property and trying to drink a cup of cold coffee all at the same time.

"About that dog," Sylvia began.

"Just a minute, dear," said Mrs Binns. She leapt back to the telephone, gabbling, "Eleven hundred on the roll in September, give or take a dozen either way, but we're hoping to get back to two dinner-sittings if the canteen extension's finished in time ..." She faced Sylvia. "He's brown, short-haired, white chest and paws, and a black bottom and long tail, and he's going to be big and need a lot of food and exercise. Terribly mixed ancestry, and a proper devil."

"I'd like him," said Sylvia, to her own astonishment. "Ask your parents ... I mean, ask your mother," said Mrs Binns, returning her attention to the telephone.

Any reminder of the divorce still made Sylvia feel sick. She stumped out of the office ungraciously. But she saw the sense in Mrs Binns's caution. Adopting any dog, let alone a proper devil, needed tact not confrontation.

A tall shape blocked the corridor. It was Philip Rowntree, pinning up the guest list for the end-of-term prize giving. He regarded her sadly.

"I hear you're leaving," he said.

"I can't see that it makes any difference to you," snapped Sylvia. "You won't be here." But she was glad he cared. Her awful news must have been a little bit important to have penetrated the sixth form.

"I'd have come to see you in *Pirates*. You never know, Dennis might have invited me back to play Frederick if he got desperate."

Philip had always sung the tenor lead opposite her, and made her feel inferior with his toffee-nosed BBC accent.

"He's giving my part to Doreen Loach."

Philip laughed. "Then I shan't be available! You look depressed. Let me get you a coffee."

They moved through double doors to an automatic drinks machine.

"I'd rather have tea."

Sylvia argued with Philip Rowntree as a matter of course because he was upper class and well-off, and usually right about everything, and his parents still lived together. But she let him buy her a plastic cup of tea and steer her out to a quiet part of the playing-field behind the tennis courts, where the threatened hay fever got the better of her.

"It's your fault," she raged at him, scrubbing her tear-stained face with a Kleenex. "You shouldn't have been kind." He held her glasses and her tea while she recovered. She drank the tea and pitched the carton into the bushes.

"People who leave litter deserve a good hiding," said Philip, mildly. "D'you feel better now?"

"Yes," sighed Sylvia. "I've been wanting to have a good howl all morning." She pitched the Kleenex into the bushes and faced him. "I expect you'll tell your friends I've been making an exhibition of myself."

"That's unlikely," said Philip.

Sylvia realized it was true. Philip had no friends in particular. He wasn't one of a crowd. He got on reasonably well with everyone, worked hard and won things. But people kept their distance. He was never any good for an aimless gossip. He looked at his watch.

"Five more minutes," he said. "Will you do me a favour?"

"Depends what it is."

"Ask me some questions on this."

He produced a copy of the Highway Code from his pocket. Sylvia flipped through the pages and tried to catch him out on road signs and what to do on motorways. He knew all the answers, typically. As they sprawled on the grass with the sun on their backs, Sylvia began to wish he was better-looking. By the time the bell rang for the end of break, she had decided that it didn't matter that he wasn't exactly gorgeous.

"When are you taking your test?"

"This afternoon. Wish me luck?"

"Of course."

He hauled her to her feet. "If I pass ... and if you'd like to give me your address before you leave ... I could drive out of London and see you sometimes." He retrieved the Kleenex and the plastic cup from the bushes, squashed them in his hand and dropped them in a waste bin as they wandered back towards the school buildings. Sylvia's thoughts were in a disorderly jumble. She dared not admit to Penny and Clare that Philip Rowntree might turn up in her life. It was all rather unexpected. Suppose he came while they were staying with her. How on earth would she explain it?

Perhaps he would fail his test. They had all split themselves laughing at him weeks ago, as he drove round and round the outskirts of the park with his L-plates on, crunching his gears, kangaroo-hopping at junctions. But they hadn't seen him recently. He'd probably been out on the dual carriageway, getting smoother and more confident every day.

"I suppose you want a cheap day out in the country," grumbled Sylvia. "I daresay I'll have a few visitors until the novelty wears off."

Philip was amused. "There's no such thing as a cheap day out with petrol the price it is. And I'd come to see you even if you were moving to an ugly dump of a place."

"I'm going out of my mind," Sylvia thought. "This isn't really happening."

"What is it you like about me?" Her voice wobbled and seemed to be forcing itself through a sieve.

"Everything except your shoes. They're hideous. And they make you walk so badly. You'll break your

48

ankles if you aren't careful. Did I hear you telling Mrs Binns you were going to have that dog?"

The argument with her mother smouldered all evening, with flare-ups when one made a point which the other could not squash completely flat.

"We're moving from London to save money, not to spend even more buying meat for a dog."

"Let me stay here with my friends, then, and I won't have a dog."

Sylvia's mother flared up. "Don't blackmail me, Sylvia. You'll make new friends."

"How?" yelled Sylvia. "Three miles from a bus route? No youth club? No disco?"

"You'll have your bike in summer, and television in winter and anyway, you'll spend most evenings doing homework while I'm out."

Sylvia's mother was to be an agent for a firm selling perfume and cosmetics at evening parties. It was a smart job, and she was looking forward to proving herself as a businesswoman. But the prospect of hasty tea times when Sylvia came home from school, and then leaving her alone in a remote cottage, were thoughts that were already niggling her with guilt. Sylvia knew, and played on it.

"Anything could happen to me," Sylvia flared up in her turn. "You'll be gone for hours, wittering away to stupid women about skin care, while I'm being burgled and murdered. I need that dog for protection!"

"When you had a guinea-pig, I always had to clean its cage."

"Mum, I was only seven!"

Sylvia sensed victory. She didn't particularly want the dog, but she did want to win, to have it recognized that she couldn't be pushed about without some compensation. As her mother wavered, Sylvia made rash promises to train the dog, to exercise the dog, to take a Saturday job and pay towards its keep; to be responsible. She won.

After school the following day, when she saw the dog, she wished she had lost and could have retreated behind a sad, "My Mum wouldn't let me!"

He was leggy. His head was too big for his wriggling body. He was a grinning, licking frolic of a dog. He bashed her legs with his white forepaws and laddered her tights. She tried him on a lead in front of the kennels. He set off like an inter-city express, then stopped suddenly and she fell over him. His muscular tail thumped bruises into her calves.

"I don't think I can manage him," she admitted.

Mrs Binns was watching her. "Better forget the idea, then," she said. "He's boisterous, but he has a lovely nature. It wouldn't do to have him ruined by a bad owner who won't trouble to bring out the best in him."

"Why should he do what you want?" Philip asked. "You haven't even bothered to give him a name yet."

Philip had driven them to the kennels. His L-plates were in the dustbin and he was enjoying the spectacle of Sylvia being towed madly in all directions against her will. She swung round on him furiously.

"Yes, I have!" she stormed. "He's called Rastus."

Philip took the lead from her. "Here, Rastus," he said. "Sit."

He stooped, pressed the dog's hindquarters down and jerked the lead firmly up. The dog, surprised, sat. The surprise lasted a couple of seconds before he stood up again and cantered off, pulling the full weight of Philip clumsily behind. Sylvia nearly collapsed laughing and had to hold on to Mrs Binns for support.

After twenty minutes, Rastus was walking soberly. Sylvia took the lead, feeling self-conscious but proud.

"He's going to be handsome," she boasted. "He's intelligent. Look how quickly he's learnt to walk to heel."

"Rubbish," said Philip breathlessly. "He's tired out, that's all. Wait until he's had a rest."

Rastus was easily persuaded into the back of the car. He sat up, poised, alert and inquisitive, as good as gold. Sylvia was enchanted.

"Well," Mrs Binns was saying, "If you're sure ... He's had his injections. You'll have to pay for those, of course, and a donation would be welcome ..."

The idea of paying money for adopting a homeless dog had not occurred to Sylvia. She thought of her small savings in the Post Office. Philip was taking banknotes from his wallet and passing them to Mrs Binns. Sylvia tried to argue, but was pushed into the passenger seat and driven home, with Rastus tranquilly blowing down the back of her neck.

"I can afford to," Philip reasoned. "Call it your leaving present if you like. That dog's a tough nut, he'll live for years, and cost you plenty. Also, he'll give you plenty of fun and affection, Sylvia, and I'd like to make a small contribution to that."

Sylvia felt choked. Leaving was going to be even more difficult now that Philip was part of what was to be left behind.

When the day of departure came, the main difficulty was Rastus. He had spent a week wrecking the house which Sylvia's divorced parents had sold, to quote the Estate Agents, "in immaculate decorative order throughout". He had dug up half the garden for the incoming new owners. Penny and Clare had both had their tights laddered and had stopped coming round to say goodbye and check that Sylvia had not packed any of their LPs by mistake. Rastus had been retrieved from the furniture van several times, and had seen off the removal men whenever they had tried to cross the threshold. When Philip drove Sylvia and her mother and Rastus to the railway station, there was a chilly atmosphere in the car. Sylvia's mother produced their tickets from her chewed handbag, and Rastus resolutely refused to get on the train.

"We should have expected this," Philip said calmly. "That dog obviously prefers cars. Railways are a bit overwhelming."

Hundreds of people with holiday luggage battled through the barrier, sidestepping, climbing over the taut lead as Rastus braced his legs and refused to move.

Sylvia's mother looked irritably at the clock.

"This is ridiculous," she snapped. "The train leaves in one minute, and if we aren't on it, the removal men will arrive before us and put all the furniture in the wrong rooms."

"Leave Rastus with me," Philip volunteered, "I'll bring him down at the weekend when you're straight."

Sylvia was swamped with gratitude. She hugged Philip, stroked the dog's ears and hustled her mother on to the train, where they both grinned at each other because they were both in tears.

"You know, love," her mother confessed, "I didn't want to leave London either. But it's a new beginning. Let's see what we can make of it."

Sylvia was simply relieved that it wasn't a final ending, that Philip would be with her at the weekend;

and she blessed Rastus for being a proper devil.

"I wonder what the new people will think of the bathroom wallpaper being ripped off and the scratches on the paintwork!" said Sylvia's mother, adding hopefully, "They're bound to redecorate anyway. Nobody ever likes an existing colour scheme." She laughed and looked shyly at her daughter. "Sylvia, I think Philip's awfully nice. You've done well there."

Sylvia blushed. "I don't know what you mean," she said. "I didn't do anything."

The cottage was shabby, unpretentious, dreaming in an overgrown garden. There wasn't a trace of new paint anywhere. Generations of dogs had already battered the old oak doors. Penny and Clare would think she'd come down in the world, and Sylvia didn't mind. Rastus would love it. There was a derelict hencoop in the orchard and Sylvia could already imagine him burrowing underneath it, chasing smells. She could almost see him, a jungle creature in the neglected vegetable garden, energetically plunging his paws into the rank compost heap. She unpacked tea chests until the sewing-machine was revealed, and began shortening curtains.

A Mrs Tuffett arrived with six brown eggs and told Sylvia's mother all about the Women's Institute. The next day, a Mr Brewster, at least seventy years of age and with no teeth, mended the chain on Sylvia's bicycle and took her back to choose cuttings from his garden. He showed her a deep, brick-lined well, once the village water supply, and some faded photographs of the old couple who had lived in her own cottage and who now lay together in the churchyard.

On the Friday evening, a Mr Adams took away the stuff they couldn't find room for in their new home, loading it on his tractor and trailer to augment the village jumble sale, and on the Saturday morning Sylvia bought two pairs of comfortable shoes there, so that she could walk the lanes with Rastus and not break her ankles.

On the Saturday afternoon, Philip arrived with the dog. Rastus behaved very well for Philip, and very badly for Sylvia.

"It'll be all right," gasped Sylvia, engaged in a tug-of-war with Rastus over a mere matter of a candlewick bedspread. "I got a leaflet from the vet, telling me what to do. Bad dog! Leave!"

Philip was coating the bedroom ceiling with emulsion paint when Rastus cannoned into the step-ladder and left Philip white-streaked and swearing on the floor. Sylvia's mother washed his trousers and shirt immediately, but he had to stay the night while they dried. He spent Sunday morning tightly constrained in a pair of Sylvia's jeans, borrowed a scythe from Mr Adams, and reduced the jungle in the garden to a manageable height.

"Come again for another restful weekend," said Sylvia bitterly, as Philip prepared to leave. She was sure that she would never see him any more.

During the next four weeks, she found every day too short. It would have been lovely to sunbathe in the garden, to close her eyes and imagine herself back with the crowd in the park, laughing and fooling about. But weeds choking the roses claimed her attention; she discovered old raspberry canes and new potatoes; there was too much to do, and the fact that she acquired a holiday suntan was incidental. She realized that friends could be people of any age. Mr Brewster told her earthy jokes she hadn't heard before, the sort which made her laugh without feeling disgusted. Mrs Tuffett was bossy and kept sending her on errands on her bike, but rewarded her with gooseberry jam and the best sponge cakes Sylvia had ever tasted.

Since the move, Sylvia's mother had begun to talk to her as an adult, even about money matters. They worked out the payments between them on the new car which was essential to the new job. Sylvia's maths came in handy. But she missed the glorious moment when her mother drove off to the challenge of a business career, as Rastus had escaped and had to be hunted for miles around and taught never to go into a field where there were cattle or sheep. "That dog!" the people in the village said. "You keep him under control, or else!"

"He is improving," Sylvia wrote in answer to a letter from Philip. "But he pleases himself about coming when he's called. I took him to a choir tea with me, and he upset the trestle table, smashed two cups and ate the buns, and when the Vicar called to meet Mum, Rastus fetched the lavatory brush and presented him with it!"

Penny and Clare had been for a long weekend, and it had been awkward. They obviously had known about the friendship with Philip, and were afraid to mention him, remembering how often they had called him a twit and a bore. Rastus had a miserable time. These visitors didn't understand that he claimed the right to sleep on any bed he chose. When the three cyclists went for a ride with Rastus lolloping behind, an old lady ticked them off, saying it was a dangerous way to exercise a dog. Then it rained, and Penny and Clare went home sooner than was planned, their holiday clothes covered with muddy pawmarks. They were sorry for Sylvia.

"You're ruining my life, Rastus," said Sylvia, smiling secretly and scratching his back. "I hate you." Rastus wriggled his appreciation and dug up the plants she had just bedded. They were both looking forward to Philip's next visit. When jokes were made between Mr Adams and Mrs Tuffett and Mr Brewster about Sylvia's young man, she just felt happy, not embarrassed.

Towards the end of August, he was really there, picnicking by the river with them, feeding bits of cheese sandwich to Rastus, telling Sylvia of the varied jobs he'd done to earn funds for university. His family was too well off for him to get a grant, and he loathed asking for handouts. His "A" level results were through, and he was mightily pleased about something.

"Which university, then?" Sylvia asked quietly, pulling seed heads off the long grasses, thinking of all the charming girl students he'd meet in some faraway city.

Philip was silent. Sylvia sipped the last of her Coca Cola out of the can as if nothing were more important.

Philip grinned sideways at her. "Southampton."

Sylvia cheered, and threw the empty can into the river with all her strength. It glinted joyously in the sun.

"You hooligan!" Philip clobbered her, quite hard. "You don't deserve to live in a place like this." He pulled a long withy stick from the overgrown bank. "Fish it out! Go on! You can't leave tin cans polluting a beautiful river!" He pushed the withy into her hand.

"I can't reach," she giggled, "I'll fall in."

"Serve you right."

The can bobbed and swerved as it sailed downstream. Sylvia chased along the bank after it. A mat of weed checked its progress. She clung to a branch of willow and leaned over, trying to coax the can towards the bank with the withy. "I still can't reach." Philip held on to the willow and secured her hand so that she could lean full stretch away from the bank and hook the can delicately out of the water.

Rastus joined the game by charging between Philip's feet. There was a squelch, and a series of splashes, as boy, girl and dog all went helplessly into the river.

Sylvia stood up, thigh-deep in water, mud oozing into her shoes, her clothes sodden, her hair dripping. Philip was wiping his face and looking concerned.

"Are you all right?"

"I've lost my glasses."

"Okay, I'll find them. You get back on the path."

He waded to where she had fallen in, and ducked half a dozen times to scan the river bed, before climbing the bank, a pair of spectacles triumphantly in his hand. He placed them in her soaking lap and sat down beside her.

"This is the moment," Sylvia thought. "And it's not a bit like it says in the magazines."

There was no orchestra, she wasn't wearing a ravishing long dress and a musky perfume. A couple of lapwings cried overhead, she was in old wet denims and stank of waterweed. She put the Coca Cola tin in Philip's lap. More water streamed out of it over his legs.

"Satisfied?" she asked.

He laughed. "Not quite," and rolled her over and kissed her.

Life was full of wonderful surprises. Sylvia would have liked the kiss to go on and on, but she sat up suddenly, bumping Philip's nose with her forehead.

"Where's Rastus?"

She needn't have asked. Rastus had discovered he

could swim. He came out of the river some while later, just as they were beginning to dry out, and shook himself all over them.

For a dog, too, life was full of surprises. Philip and Sylvia didn't seem in a mood to scold him at all.

Freda Kelsall ran a children's library and taught before becoming a writer. As a TV dramatist her work includes two popular series for schools: How We Used To Live, 1874–1887, *and* 1908–1945. *She has had four books for children published, and one adult novel, a satire on the controversy over Shakespeare's real identity. Her current interests are in rural communities and the National Trust. She has lived in a northern seaside resort, an airy part of London, and the Hampshire countryside.*

LOVE AND BE DAMNED

Petronella Breinburg

"Take that ... and that ... and this." I kicked the side of my sister's scooter. I'd ridden it before, so why the hell was it giving me trouble now, eh? The devil I suppose! But then I *was* running off with someone from Devil's Island.

I kicked the starter again, but nothing happened. Oh, trust me, trust Lucia van Duiker to get stranded on a lonely road at four o'clock in the morning. But when else could I run off? And how could I wait for a bus? Anyone would remember me. My dad and uncle were so well known in St Laurence. How could I escape unseen?

Maybe if I went through that lane. It did look dark, but it would keep me from the main road. At least by the main road I could get a lift from someone who was a stranger to St Laurence. People do travel backwards and forwards between Cayene and St Laurence.

Again I tried to start the engine, again no luck. It was as if something evil, maybe a devil, was trying to stop me going away. But what else could I do? My family would never accept Pierre. He was a descendant of people sent to Devil's Island from Europe. "Worst criminals from Europe came to Devil's Island," so my wise uncle kept saying. My argument that this was centuries ago, and had nothing to do with my Pierre, went to deaf ears.

Then, when at last I announced that Pierre and I

were engaged to be married, all hell let loose.

"Over my dead body," my father roared. My mother fainted, my sister dashed off to the kitchen. Mama Mathilda, the woman who looked after us children from the day we were born, rushed off to the bathroom for bay rum to rub my mother down.

My uncle was the one who swore he'd shoot Pierre. He hadn't been in the army for nothing. He had killed many Germans in the Second World War, so he claimed anyway. He wouldn't hesitate to kill a young rascal, and grandson of criminals, who tried to seduce his niece.

Pierre ran for his life and went into hiding. But I knew where he was. I was to meet him and together we'd escape somehow — to Brazil, where they wouldn't find us. We wouldn't dare go in the other direction, to Surinam. That was where all my relations were — the first place my dad would look for us. In fact, my relations wouldn't keep us at all. Never! No one in Surinam would let their daughter marry a man from French Guyana, those descendants from Europe's worst criminals.

I pushed my sister's scooter through Crowly Lane, thinking over the whole of my story with Pierre, from that first day we met at that High School festival, until now, two years later. After a while I came to what looked like an old burial ground, now being cleared for houses to be built on.

I went on thinking: We're not even allowed to speak to these people; how stupid! Why then did Dad take a post as border policeman at the Surinam-French Guyana border? Worse still, why did he live in St Laurence, on the French side, rather than Albina, on the Dutch side of the border? And what made them think that love makes allowances for things like your background?

So busy was I, thinking of our plight, that I didn't look where I was going. When suddenly I noticed a shape in front of me, I thought that the moon was playing one of its tricks. This often happens. It happens particularly with plantain trees. They've got this habit of appearing like human shapes against the moonlight.

I tried to laugh. I remembered the many tales Mama Mathilda used to tell us. Shapes of plantain trees had made people run from fright, thinking they were ghosts.

But I did not succeed in laughing, because when I looked round, I noticed that there was not a single tree around. There were one or two tombs. Some were those big ones like houses, in which French Generals and other officials who had died while guarding the prisoners were buried. Mind you, not many French officials were buried there because most of them, when dead, had been flown back to Europe. Something to do with French Guyana being unsuited, because the many prisoners and shot slaves who were haunting the place made the ground unholy for decent folk.

Oh come on. You're not scared, are you? I kidded myself and continued to push my bike along. The bike felt very heavy now. Maybe I was going up hill. I was not sure. I didn't know that part of St Laurence very well. I only knew the main road, and the monuments my father had taken me to. What little courting Pierre and I did had been done on my school paths, and so on.

The shadow seemed to come closer. Or was I just walking towards it? I looked to my right to see if I could turn another way, and so avoid passing that shadow. Of course, I thought, I'm not afraid of no silly shadow. There must be a simple explanation for it. Maybe Pierre had decided to meet me after all. But how could he know I'd leave home so early? I'd told him I'd be on my way at six, on the six o'clock bus. It was a last minute thing that I took my sister's scooter. Oh, the scooter! But my sister or father couldn't have tampered with it, because they didn't know I was going to take it. Or did they? My father always says that I'm so much like my mother that he can almost predict what I'll do next. Maybe he had suspected and tampered with the scooter? And now he was standing somewhere waiting for me. That shadow was my dad's!

Once I had decided that it was my father in the semi-darkness, I pushed the scooter angrily towards the shadow. Suddenly I realized that something was wrong. I was taking too long to reach the shadow. It was as if it was moving away while I moved forward. "That's it!" I thought. "It wants me to follow it, or something."

Ah, some man dressed up in a cloak; that's what it looked like. Wonder if it's a living person? My dad wouldn't want to frighten the life out of me.

Oh, my God! Not a murderer, or worse still, a rapist! "I'll kick his shin bone in," I said to myself. "But what makes you think it's a he? Could it be a woman? A female ghost? Or Mama Mathilda trying to scare me back home?" Well, Mama Mathilda was wasting her time. My mind was made up. If Pierre couldn't come to me without being shot by my uncle, I'd go to him, shadow or no shadow ... I took a deep breath, gathered all the strength into my arms and legs, and pushed the scooter up towards the shadow. This time it didn't move back. It was waiting for me to get to the top of that hill.

I saw him clearly then. It was, so it appeared anyway, a young man. I saw his feet first, as I went up the hill. He had sandals on. His trousers were white, lily or milky-white, too white for such a dusty road. His shirt was an open-necked one, more like a sort of ceremonial gown than a shirt. The shirt sleeves were long, and I couldn't see his hands at all, not at first anyway. His neck had a sort of chain round it. A chain with a pendant dangling from it. Then I saw his face, and let go of the scooter. I had never seen such a pale face. It was as if every ounce of blood had drained from it. I'd never actually seen a dead person, but I'd heard my dad say after he had helped fish a dead body out of the river near us: "It was white and bloodless, white as a fish."

The whiteness before me was not a nice one. It was one which frightened me. Then I thought: "Someone has a white mask on. Someone who is trying to scare me." But to be on the safe side, I took two steps backwards while telling myself that I was not afraid.

"I'm not afraid of you, whoever you are!" I said, hoping that I'd convince the figure. It took a step towards me.

I took a further step or two back. The figure came towards me without even seeming to move. It was as if it was attached to my body by a magnet, so that every step I took it went along with me.

"He'll kill me!" I thought, and suddenly visualized myself lying in a pool of blood. I was sure now that he was some sort of escaped convict. There had been things in the papers about escaped convicts from nearby countries, hiding in French Guyana.

"Scream! Scream, you fool!" a voice seemed to shout at me through the wind. But though I actually screamed, no sound came out. If it had I would have heard it, even with the strange whistling of the wind. My throat felt dry as if something was choking me and trying to stop me screaming.

"Run! Run! Run back! Run!" Again I seemed to hear voices shouting these things. I ran, or tried to, but my feet were heavy, like blocks of lead, and refused to move.

Maybe if I was nice and friendly he'd let me go. So I forced a smile on to my face and said: "Hello. Nice morning ..."

Then I saw his eyes. I hadn't noticed them before. They were hidden beneath long eyelashes which made his face look as if it had two hairy slits where his eyes should have been.

The hairy eyes moved from my face to my chest. I could feel them boring holes into my breast. I remembered the stories we'd read. "If attacked, all they want is your money or your jewels. Give, without any argument." I had no money except a few cents. But I did have a gold chain with a locket in which I had Pierre's picture. I also had my Piet-piet earring given to me by Mama Dika, my Godmother, when I first menstruated.

"Here, have this, and this, and this ..." I began peeling the things off and handing them over. But the man made no attempt to take them. I dropped them at his feet. "My dad, he's the police commissioner. You harm me and you'll be caught, no matter where you go. And my uncle, Danny, he's been in the army. He can shoot a fly off your nose ..." I felt myself swaying. I felt very faint and pleaded: "Please don't, please ..." Those were the last words I heard myself whispering before my head hit the hard clay road.

I came to, or rather the smell of garlic brought me to. The smell was different from any smell I'd come across before. I tried not to open my eyes. I told myself that if I pretended to be dead, he'd leave me and go away. Suddenly I thought that maybe I was dead. Maybe this was how it smelled in Heaven, or wherever dead people went.

I heard voices, but they were speaking in a language I didn't know. I knew it wasn't French because I did French at school and I would have understood. It wasn't even Patois, not the one spoken in St Laurence anyway. I could understand that a little bit. It wasn't Sranan-tongo either. That's the language spoken by Surinam's Creole, especially those living alongside the Albina river.

Someone touched my hand. The person began to rub some smelly stuff on my face.

Slowly I began to open my eyes. Somehow, I felt that these were friendly people. When I finally opened my eyes fully, I noticed that these people were like Indians. It was a motherly looking woman who was rubbing my face. She stopped rubbing when she noticed that I had regained consciousness.

"Thank you," I said, because I didn't know what else to say.

But the people didn't understand me. I remembered then that even in Surinam, villagers and river people did not understand my city and high-school Dutch. You had to speak Sranan-tongo to them. So I thought that perhaps here it would be the same. These village, or mountain people, would not understand the French I had learned at school, so I tried speaking my little bit of Patois.

But again, no sign of understanding.

So I smiled. My dad always said that a friendly smile can work wonders.

It was then that a young girl, about my age, or perhaps a few months older, which would have made her sixteen and a half, came up. She must have been learning Dutch at school and she spoke to me haltingly:

"My brother found you. He was going to work. We brought you here. We are *mountaines* ..." said the young girl, in very poor Dutch.

I wasn't sure what *mountaines* were, but I nodded my head and pretended that I did.

"Something frightened you?"

"Oh, yes, a man. Or was that your brother?"

The girl translated to the older people before she spoke to me again.

"No, you had already fainted when he came by."

"Oh!" Fear came over me again. What had happened between the time I had fainted and been found? How long had I been unconscious?

The girl must have read my mind because she said, "Were you lost? Where do you wish to go? We'll take you to your people."

"I'm going to a place called Rene."

"Rene?" The girl looked alarmed.

"Yes."

"Not a very nice place, I must tell you!" The girl looked nervously at me and then at her elders.

"I must go there. I must meet, er, my fiancé there."

"Fiancé?" The girl didn't know the word.

"Yes. That's someone I'm going to marry."

The girl translated to her elders. They spoke to her. She translated to me.

"What happened? What frightened you?"

"A man, a shape, then, well, it looked like a man. He got my jewels."

"These?" The girl took a callabas and showed it to me. All my things were intact.

"But, I thought he was a thief!" Again, an ugly fear came into my mind.

"What did he look like?"

I described the horrible face and the girl explained

66

it to her elders. They didn't seem to share my nervousness about that apparition.

"That's Wajoema you've seen. He wanted you to turn back," the girl explained.

"Wajoema?"

"Yes, Wajoema. You're lucky. Only lucky people see Wajoema."

"Who's he?"

"He protects us. Warns us of danger. You're running away, yes?"

"How do you know?"

"Wajoema, so the story is told, was a runaway."

"A runaway?"

"Yes, a runaway from Devil's Island. He was hunted like a wild animal."

"What happened? Was he caught?"

"He was, because he fell in love and married a *mountaine* girl. He stayed here, and he got caught."

"Oh." I got to my feet. I was ready to leave.

"You must go back to your own people. You'll be caught if you don't."

"Well, I shall have to be caught!" I said, determined to get to Pierre.

"No! You must go back. Never go forward if Wajoema says, no!"

"I must go forward ... I must get to Rene by eight o'clock."

The girl conferred with her elders. They spoke in whispers, perhaps forgetting that I could not understand what was being said.

They spoke to the girl, who then passed it on to me: "Very well. My brother and uncle will take you." The girl looked at me as if she was sorry for me.

For a moment I thought that we would be going on a bus, or a cart of some kind, then I realized that we would be going on foot.

Nor did I realize how far away Rene was, or that Rene was no more than a little settlement with about six huts. Somehow, before I even asked, I knew it:

"Pierre has gone to St Laurence," a woman told me. "He hates it here, he's gone."

"How long ago?" I felt as if iced water had been poured over me.

"Three days, maybe more. But why not ask his wife?"

Those words killed me. I became a zombie, just wandering along.

Walking back to the *mountaines* was easier. Going down the hill was easier than going up. My sister's scooter was still on its side where I had left it. I kicked the engine. It started at once. No trouble at all, none whatsoever. There was nothing wrong with the scooter, never had been, unless someone had repaired it while I had been gone.

I rode back home, to my relations, my dad, my uncle and sister, Mama Mathilda.

Wajoema, Pierre, Rene, were far away, very far away.

Petronella Breinburg is an ex-teacher who hails from Surinam in South America. She has published a number of books for young people and her short stories and articles appear in several anthologies. Much of her unpublished work is used by minority groups such as adult illiterates, non-English speakers, etc.

She is at present doing research and is attached to the Education department of the University of Keele.

HORIZONS

Sam McBratney

As soon as Michael asked her to go to the rugby club
dance, Lynn knew her mother was the one she had to
convince. "You want to go to a formal dance? And
you're not even seventeen? Well I don't know about
that. What does your father say?"

Her elder brother Gordon gave his awful oafish
laugh again and her father said, "I suppose she's got
to get used to the ways of the world sooner or later."

"Let it be later then," replied mother. "The ways
of the world are soon enough got used to for one not
left school a year."

From then on, it was a matter of being especially
helpful about the house, and of being tactful in her
answers to a multitude of questions about the coming
event. Who was he anyway, she wanted to know? A
rugby player! They were the worst kind. Did she know
his people? No, so he could be anybody. What age
was he? Eighteen! They'd no sense at eighteen,
especially if he was a student? Yes, she thought so,
and with a flat of his own, no doubt. And did he
smoke, did he drive, and did he drink much when
they were out together?

It was the question of alcohol that bothered her
mother most, so Lynn was very careful with her
answer.

"Look, mummy," she said patiently, "He drinks
very little – he has to play rugby. If it's drink you
want to see, go down to the disco where it isn't even

on sale. Half of them are drunk and you don't make a fuss about me going there." "No, but you're with girl friends. You're not dancing with one boy the whole night. I don't like to think of you dancing with one person all the night long, it's too serious."

But Lynn managed to swing it her way in the end. It helped when she admitted that she wasn't all that keen on Michael anyway, it was more the occasion she was going for.

On the night of the dance she got picked up at her front door by the eighteen-year-old rugby player who shook hands with her parents and promised to have her back on the dot of one-thirty. Her long dress rustled as she walked down the path, and when she paused at the door of his car to gather up the folds and slip into his front seat, it was like a movement rehearsed a thousand times. Her mother watched her departure from the door, her father from behind a curtain inside the house.

Her mother said: "Isn't she awfully young?"

"It'll broaden her horizons," her father said. "That's only the front path out there, not the aisle."

The house that night seemed empty without Lynn, even though she was usually out on a Friday. Her parents sat watching the television through to the end of programmes. Gordon came in at about twelve o'clock and wondered out loud how Cinderella was getting on.

"Now you give over," he got told by his mother, "and leave her alone. And don't torture her tomorrow and have her in tears with your talk, you hear ..."

They didn't wait up for her to come in, but for all the sleep she got through worrying about Lynn, her mother might just as well have done. She couldn't understand how her husband in the bed beside her could get to sleep so quick and sound with his only daughter out in the wee small hours and "broadening her horizons" as he put it. She couldn't even remember which hotel the dance was at. At a quarter past two she had it in her mind to waken him and ask him when she heard the key in the lock.

She was quickly out of bed and to the head of the stairs. Some giggling reached her, then quiet.

Should she speak down to them or not? It might be just as well to let them know she knew they were back.

"Are you there, Lynn?"

A pause, then,

"Yes, mummy, Michael's just going. I'll be up in a minute or two."

"Just put the chain on the door, dear."

Back in bed she counted the minutes. About eight of them went by before she heard the sound of his car leaving the street, and she was able to content herself with the fact that the dance was over.

She wondered if the next few years were going to be difficult with Lynn. Somehow boys weren't the same. She didn't worry about Gordon so much, and anyway, he hadn't the same life and spirit in him to go to these places.

When Lynn woke the next morning and swung her feet out of bed, she sat for a moment and wondered how her head was so clear and her body so fresh after the activities of the night before. She'd hardly been off her feet the whole time, except during the meal, and getting through that heap of food had been like a day's work.

It was twelve-thirty by the clock on the dressing-table. Lynn skipped down the stairs to the phone.

"Is that you, Lynn?" she heard her mother shout. "Lunch!"

"In a minute, mummy. I'm just phoning Gillian if she's in."

There was no "if" about it. Lynn knew Gillian would be in and waiting for every pick of news.

"Well Gillian, I went! Yes. No, listen, I'm in the hall. *Five* babychams. Well it's a lot for *me* Gillian, you know how I giggle and go on. Shh! I'm only in the hall, they'll hear me. If they knew what state Michael was in driving me home I swear they'd kill me, Gillian, they would, stone dead. Uhuh. The only thing is Michael's not bad but I'd rather you-know-who had asked me. I know he's not in the rugby club but that doesn't stop you *going*, Gillian. But he was nice though, a big lamb. Uhuh. He went out once, I think to throw up but he wasn't the only one and one of them stripped down to his underpants — yes! The big hairy thing. Then he got up on the piano and started playing with his bare *feet*, Gillian you should have been there. No, I didn't know anybody — wait, I tell a lie, once I turned a corner and there was this gorgeous-looking creature in front of me in a turquoise evening dress. No Gillian, it was me in a mirror. Sort of to one side, you know that classical look, my hair seemed to do whatever I told it, you know that sort of way? Uhuh. Oh, lovely, veal cutlets. The tableware was out of this world. My people are so working class Gillian, honest to God, it was like another way of life to be sitting there cutting up all kinds of everything with a hundred different knives and forks. I had to show him which to use first. He hadn't a clue, Gillian, honestly, men know nothing. Next time I'll go with a middle-aged divorcé with grey temples. Atmosphere, it's all atmosphere, Gillian you should have been there. Yes. Uhuh. I hear them shouting at me for lunch. I'll come round later on. 'Bye."

Preparations for lunch were well advanced when Lynn made an entrance into the kitchen. Her mother smiled, asked if she'd had a nice time but didn't press for details. Her father said lightly that she was going to bed early that night so's she'd be down for breakfast the next morning.

Lynn didn't feel hungry as she sat down at the table. A loaf, half out of its plastic cover, spilled in slices on to the table, and at each of four places the lettuce leaves of a humble salad flounced over the edges of a plate to skirt the surface of a rather soiled cloth. The old and battered tea-pot, favoured for its easy pour, squatted in its accustomed place at the centre of the table.

It was all so haphazard, so totally familiar! As she watched her mother trying to do a hundred things at once, Lynn wondered if she would ever be dominated by her own kitchen.

"How's your boyfriend, then?" Her ridiculous brother started his senseless banter before he even sat down. Lynn knew better than to get angry. So far as Gordon was concerned, that was the main object of the game. He was such a big child for someone attending a polytechnic.

"Mummy, have you a clean spoon for the sugar? This one's caked hard and lumpy."

"Fussy, aren't we?" Gordon chipped in.

Lynn ignored him, of course, but in actual fact there was a lot to be fussy about. Because she wasn't hungry herself, Lynn seemed to notice all the more the way her father chewed with his mouth open, the flecks of burnt toast on the butter, the filthy thick glar round the cap of the sauce bottle.

"Just a cup of tea for me, mummy, please," Lynn said. "I'm just not very hungry at the moment."

After lunch Gordon went to play tennis with some

unsuspecting girl who couldn't possibly know what he was really like. Lynn told her parents some of the more innocent happenings of her night out, and then, in her serious voice, she said,

"Actually there is something I'd like to discuss with you."

There followed a considerable silence, broken by an "Oh?" from her mother, the non-committal sound of one who is not sure that she wants to hear more.

"Speak up, love," said her father. "There's only your mum and me and the kitchen sink."

"Well, it's just that I don't like the way we eat."

Her mother lifted one or two dishes from the table and carried them to the sink. Her father looked at her hard, and rather grimly.

"Mother, she doesn't like the way we eat."

"So I hear. Ask her what's wrong with it."

"What's wrong with what we eat?"

"It's very hard to put into words."

"Try," her father said dryly, "I'm sure you'll manage."

Lynn chose to address the milk jug as if she was getting answers from it. She had not anticipated that she would feel embarrassed.

"It's not *what* we eat, it's how. It's got ... no atmosphere."

"Mother, our eating's got no atmosphere in it," her father echoed, and Lynn, blushing, rushed to her own defence.

"I don't mean we should have endless curries and fancy cheeses and veal cutlets all the time — it's *how* we eat, it's so ... *plain*."

With her hands buried in the depths of the tea-towel, Lynn's mother faced her daughter. She stood with her head askance, as if to discover some other

74

meaning in what she had just heard.

"What else do you not like about us?" she asked.

Lynn shook her head, trying to indicate that this was not what she'd meant or what she'd intended to happen.

"Maybe we should change the way we talk, too?" her mother went on regardless.

"No!" Lynn said, frightened by how big the issue had become in the space of a few sentences. "Daddy it's not fair, I didn't mean it like that."

"It sounds fair to me," her father said. "I think you've got a bloody nerve, if you want to know."

Lynn, by no means a child but still not a woman, looked her in-between self as she fought back tears of resentment at her parents' misunderstanding, which seemed almost deliberate. The responsibility of standing there and defending her position seemed altogether too much for her. Rather than take on both of them at once, she left the room.

The mother looked at the father, whose face showed the dilemma going on in his mind: whether to feel peeved or angry.

"So much for broad horizons," she said in a matter-of-fact way.

The adversaries in this word battle did not meet again until tea-time, when the family gathered once more round the kitchen table, to eat. Gordon was totally bewildered by what went on. His mother wore her necklace of imitation pearls as she uncorked a bottle of wine and delivered a slurp into each of four glasses. His father, wearing the overalls he'd been painting in, spread a linen napkin over his knee and said of the wine: "Delicate." Lip-lip-lip-lip, smack-smack. "Dry." Lip-lip, smack-smack. "And delightful. It takes a white wine for fish, what do you think, Lynn?"

Gordon was amazed that his sister had nothing to say, for there was a talking point no matter where he looked. The candle for a start, with its guttering flame! He lifted one of the heavy, pearl-handed knives lying by his plate and balanced it on a finger. Every piece of cutlery on the table matched its fellow.

"Lah-dee-dah," Gordon said. "Are we expecting the Queen?" He was told ever so politely to mind his own business when he inquired if father had won the pools. When he looked to Lynn for a sign that he'd come to the right house for his tea, she was sitting with her head down.

Gordon asked when they all seemed ready to start, "Is it this knife here?"

"You start at the outside and work in," his mother told him, "as you know rightly."

"One day, my lad," said his father, "if you work hard, you might join the ranks of the aristocrockery. We don't want to be disgraced, do we Lynn? Lynn?"

"Yes, that's right," Lynn said with some hostility.

" 'He was only a foreman's son,' they'll say, 'but he picked up every pea on his fork.' "

The rest of Lynn's Saturday night passed rapidly by. First, Michael phoned and had to be told that she wasn't able to go out after coming in late the night before. Then she was asked to do the dishes so that her mother could see the detective show on TV for a change. It took her a full hour, for every dish in the house seemed to have been used in the preparation of the four course meal, and every single knife, fork and spoon had to be thoroughly dried and slotted into a special box with a satin finish inside. Willingly, she went to bed early.

The last person she saw that day was Gordon, who

gave a timid little knock on her door and came in.

"What is going on in this house?" he asked, subdued for once.

"Nothing," said Lynn.

"They were okay when I left them at lunch. Then I arrive back to the Mad Hatter's tea party. Do you know what they're doing now? They're down there slugging the rest of their wine and watching Dracula."

"I criticized their eating habits," Lynn said quietly. "I said it was a bit plain, it didn't have any style."

Gordon took a few moments to fit this information into what he already knew of the day's events. Eventually, he got it. It shocked Lynn to see how seriously Gordon took her confession. Normally everything was a big joke to him.

"So that's it! You mean ... because of what you said, they went straight out and bought all that table stuff? They need their heads examined."

On his way out, Gordon flicked off her light just to annoy her.

"And where did the old man get the money for it all?" his silhouette said from the door. "He's always pleading poverty, says he hasn't two pennies to rub together. He'll not have now, that's for sure."

"Switch on my light," Lynn snapped at him.

"Switch it on yourself," he said. "Snob!"

Lying there in the dark above the morbid music of the late night horror film, Lynn went twenty-four hours back in time to see herself sitting at the long dining table in turquoise blue like a nervous little girl being inspected at the Guides. She'd known the knives and forks in theory, but among those confidently talking people she'd fumbled and waited for Michael's lead. She remembered with shame her impulse to let people know her age so that they could make allowances for her.

Lynn made a silent promise to herself. When she became a woman, she vowed, she would do things in style, and if that made her a snob, then too bad.

Meanwhile, in the living room below her, a happy evening was in progress. The level of wine in the continental bottle had been lowered well below the label, and a nostalgic argument was in progress. He swore it had been Great-Aunt Queenie, but she insisted that she ought to know, for her own bridesmaid Joanna had bought her the beautiful set of cutlery which for twenty years had seemed much too grand to use.

Sam McBratney: "Grew up in Lisburn in Northern Ireland. Played all kinds of sports. Chess is my outstanding hobby.

"Married with three children who are often my first critics. Since my first book, Mark Time, *I have published a book a year, including* The Final Correction, *a science fiction story, and a book of short stories for adults. I have also had a radio play broadcast.*

"I was mainly a teacher for fifteen years, and did some writing. Now I'm a writer who does some teaching. Awarded a bursary by the Northern Ireland Arts Council in 1978."

THIS ISN'T VERONA!

Joan Salvesen

I remember the first time I saw Nalini. I had been sent to the art room with a message for Mrs Savage – I've forgotten what it was.

The Upper Sixth art class were doing an exam to practise for their "A" level. They were bent over their desks, sketching busily, now and again stopping to look up at the slight figure in green posed on a central table. She sat cross-legged, the flimsy chiffon sari draped in graceful folds revealing a pair of thonged sandals, slender olive hands holding an open book, and a clearly-defined profile.

She didn't have much jewellery – just long dangling ear-rings and a necklace of golden coins. Her hair was taken back smoothly from her forehead and was veiled by the upward sweep of the sari.

She looked sideways, startled by the interruption, as I came forward and whispered to Mrs Savage who frowned impatiently and nodded her head. I stood staring at Nalini; I felt half admiring, half envious ... her skin was flawless, her silky black lashes framed eyes like a fawn's, and her parted lips were full and sensuous, a contrast to her delicate features. Everything hung together perfectly. I could understand why Mrs Savage had chosen her as a model. She was big on ethnic themes, and Nalini was just about the loveliest Indian girl I had ever seen.

One of the boys winked at me. I blushed and, turning hurriedly, went to the door. Before I closed it carefully behind me I looked back at the table. Nalini had resumed her pose, an exotic splash of colour in the grudging spring sunshine. I wondered whether we would meet again. I was curious — fascinated in an odd sort of way. Perhaps I was just bored by the pressure of approaching mock "O" levels, and she represented novelty. I guessed she was about my age, although I hadn't seen her in any of our assemblies.

Mrs Savage glared ominously in my direction and I closed the door and went off down the chilly corridor.

We met again three days later. It was a grey Monday, the sky matching the slates on the roofs and a fine drizzle penetrating clothing insidiously. I switched on the lights and sat down at my desk, snagging my new tights as I stretched my legs underneath it. I muttered in irritation and took out my copy of *Romeo and Juliet*. Miss Henley took up her copy and said hoarsely, "We'll go on with scene two — where we stopped last lesson. Benvolio's and Romeo's entrances, please."

Her cold had got worse over the weekend. Her eyes were red-rimmed and her nose shone like a polished carnelian. I listened abstractedly as the two boys read their parts. They weren't very good. I wondered whether I would be chosen to read Juliet; if there was anything I particularly enjoyed it was reading aloud, and I did it well, too.

There was a quiet tap at the door and Miss Henley croaked, "Come in."

"Ah, yes — Nalini isn't it? I heard that you'd be joining us today." She paused. "Class, this is Nalini Das Gupta."

The vision in green chiffon had gone. In her place was a conventional English schoolgirl in a denim skirt and navy sweat-shirt. Her long black hair was caught back by a tortoise-shell clasp; she wore tights in a shade of grey and her shoes were black and buckled.

"There's a free seat over there."

She slid in next to me and placed her bulging canvas bag on the floor — obviously a keen student if the contents of that bag were anything to go by.

Nalini was given the part of Juliet, to my disappointment, but I put all I had into that of the Nurse. It was really quite meaty. Nalini had a soft, slightly sibilant voice, with no trace of an Indian accent. I had to admit that she suited the part of Juliet much better than I did. I'd never imagined the fair Capulet as a large, buxom, blue-eyed Anglo-Saxon blonde!

We walked home together at the end of school. Our ways parted just beyond Fortune Green. Nalini lived with her parents and grandmother above a small and well patronised store which kept open until late in the evening; they had recently acquired it from a relative who had moved to a larger shop in Belsize Park. My home was about half a mile further on — a mock Gothic Vicarage, shabby, rambling and lined with groaning shelves of books from ground floor to attic.

I had taken over the attic when my brother had left for Cambridge. My widowed father accepted my move with a grateful smile; now he could sit at his desk and write letters to the papers on the ecumenical movement without being plagued by the sound of my records. We shared a variety of tastes but rock music wasn't one of his enthusiasms. Mrs Starling, the daily woman, had promised never to touch my attic, and she kept her promise. Occasionally my father would make his way up there and stand in the open doorway, running his fingers through his grey hair, until it stood up on end, muttering about the "state of the room" and the pressing needs of the Church's forthcoming jumble sale.

Soon Nalini became a frequent visitor although she never stayed very long. I was puzzled by this at first; all my other friends used to lounge around, drinking coffee and talking, until guilty consciences drove them back home to their books. Perhaps Nalini was more painstaking; her prep was always done on time and she was way ahead in most subjects, particularly languages.

It was quite a shock to me when I discovered the real reason for her swift departures. Her parents had forbidden her to have any social contact with people outside their own circle. Our friendship had become so important to her that, for the first time in her life, she was prepared to go behind their backs. She confessed this to me one day when I asked when I might meet them. She sat on my divan, her head hanging and her cheeks burning, as she told me.

I'd thought myself quite knowledgeable about the ways of the world – after all my father's activities had brought a wide variety of people into our home, from alcoholics drying out to ex-prisoners on probation, as well as austere Buddhist monks in saffron robes and heavily bearded Greek Orthodox priests. We'd once had a party of German boys from a remand home staying with us. Ostensibly they were meant to dig our garden and those of neighbouring OAPs. I'd volunteered to join them in the digging – my colloquial German improved enormously, but it wasn't the kind I could have used at school! I had certainly met a lot of different people and they'd all been very friendly – I'd never been treated as a bad influence before. I think I was rather hurt by the Das Guptas' attitude and, being hurt, was not inclined to search for the reasons behind it, until it was too late.

Well if Nalini wasn't allowed to invite me home I was determined to see as much of her as I could – on my own territory. And so I continued to make her welcome, whenever she could make an excuse to cover her absence, until the Vicarage became a second home to her.

It was just before our "O" levels that Mark came down for a long weekend. The wallflowers were heady with their subtle scent and the first of the lilac had come into bloom in a sheltered corner of the garden. Nalini was wearing an old pair of jeans that she kept to change into, briefly, while she was visiting me – my own would have been miles too big for her. Her family had gone away to spend the day with her married brother in Southall, and had left some friends in charge of the store (I don't think they ever took a proper holiday). The friends were a newly married couple who were too wrapped up in each other to notice Nalini's departure; according to Nalini they probably wouldn't notice her return either. There was a side entrance to the flat and she had sneaked out unobserved.

We were lying on the grass chatting about school, music, boys – all the usual things – when I heard a shout from the open French windows of the sitting room. Mark was standing there, looking very sunburned and happy to be home.

"Come and meet Devi," he said.

He performed the introductions, "Devi Ramaswamy – my sister; her friend, Nalini Das Gupta."

Apparently they had met on the train to Kings Cross, got talking and found they lived not far from each other in West Hampstead. Mark had an ability to make friends easily; he'd invited Devi to share a taxi with him, and they had decided to have a couple of cold beers together before parting.

I took stock of Devi while Mark fetched the beer. He was short and wiry, a lot darker than Nalini – almost mahogany coloured – and his teeth were startlingly white against his skin when he smiled, which he did quite often. He was studying for a diploma in Business Studies at the Technical College in Cambridge, and had come home for his sister's wedding. Like Nalini he had been born in England, although both families had come from India to settle here.

Nalini was unusually shy and said little, although she gave a fleeting smile when Mark made one of his awful jokes. To my surprise she left earlier than I had expected – I felt quite put out; I'd been looking forward to a long, lazy afternoon in the garden. Soon there wouldn't be much time for relaxation with exams hanging over us like a black cloud. Perhaps she hadn't liked Devi, although I couldn't see why. It wasn't Mark; she had met him once or twice before and they'd got on well together.

Nalini was different from the other girls – she was rather aloof with boys. There was always a hint of reserve, a sense of withdrawal, just as if she didn't dare allow herself to relax. She had never gone out with any of them, not even the Indian sixth formers who had asked her to parties and discos.

Devi left soon afterwards and I settled down to a good long chat with Mark. He took me out for a Chinese meal that evening (having borrowed the money from Dad) and I forgot all about Devi and my disappointment at Nalini's abruptness.

Two weeks to go! I was beginning to feel tense and anxious – these were my first public exams and I wasn't sure whether I'd done enough work to turn in a creditable performance. Nalini had become almost a stranger — reticent and distant. Her eyes had dark circles under them and she seemed to have grown thinner.

I supposed she was burning the candle at both ends, helping in the store after school and studying until late at night. She was ambitious, she was talented; she'd do well if she didn't get into a panic. Once or twice I caught myself watching her carefully — she was like a moth fluttering near a flame. She had that trapped look and her vivacity when it showed was febrile and excited.

We still sat next to each other in class but our exchanges were commonplace; the pleasant air of intimacy had gone and it was mostly about work that we spoke. We had our final lesson on Shakespeare, and when it was over we packed our books and files away in near silence.

When I got home I had a long cool drink — it was sultry and humid with a hint of thunder — and helping myself to an apple from the fruit bowl I went up to the attic and threw myself on the divan. I opened *Romeo and Juliet* at random. It didn't look familiar and paging back I saw that I had Nalini's copy. There was a battered postcard marking a place in the text — the kind you can buy at museums. It showed a young woman in a saffron coloured sari, on a swing suspended from the ceiling. She was being waited on by five female attendants, and looked remarkably like Nalini. The setting was very dramatic — white marble columns in a sort of colonnade. The sky beyond showed turbulent grey clouds and wind-tossed white birds.

I held the card in my hand, while I looked at some lines in the book which had been heavily underlined:

And she steal love's sweet bait from fearful hooks:
Being held a foe, he may not have access
To breathe such vows as lovers us'd to swear ...
They weren't the lines I would have chosen to
commit to memory for the exam, but English
Literature is very subjective. I flipped the card over
and my attention was caught by one name, written
again and again in Nalini's familiar handwriting —
Devi. The ink was blotched in several places.

Devi. What did he have to do with Nalini? As far
as I knew they had never met again. I decided to
probe further when I returned to school on Monday;
even if Nalini clammed up I'd get it out of her.

But she wasn't there on Monday. Miss Henley had
a statement to make.

"I'm sorry to tell you all that Nalini Das Gupta
won't be coming back again. No —" she added when
a chorus of questions arose, "she won't be taking the
exams. She is flying out to Calcutta next week to get
married."

Married! There was an incredulous murmur
around the classroom.

Miss Henley tried to explain, "Apparently her
parents had always meant her to marry someone from
their part of the world. It's what is known as an
arranged marriage. They fixed on a suitable
bridegroom about two months ago. No, he's not
ancient, only about thirty and he has a business of his
own in Calcutta. Met him before? No, I don't believe
so — it's not customary you know."

She continued the discussion during our English
lesson. She was obviously acutely aware of that empty
seat. She had borrowed a number of postcards from
Mrs Savage to help illustrate her points. They had a
lot to do with erotic love, particularly concerning the
god, Krishna, and his love for his favourite, Radha.

86

Amongst the cards was that of the young woman on the swing.

"Note the swing — it's an old Indian theme and symbolizes love menaced by threatening clouds."

I swallowed hard and remembered that one word Devi, repeated again and again ... and every time I looked at Krishna leading Radha possessively to his couch, I thought of Nalini and her new husband-to-be. My misery must have shown on my face because Miss Henley addressed herself to me personally.

"I'm sure Nalini will be very happy. Her mother told me that he is a very worthy young man, and kind. Besides she has been brought up to expect it."

Miss Henley was about fifty so perhaps she thought thirty was young. I didn't think Nalini would have agreed with her.

Outside a heavy fall of snow had deadened our footsteps, and we left a powdering of white on each carpeted stair tread. Before I had time to knock someone flung open the door and I was almost overpowered by the noise and laughter, and the smells. Rich smells of Indian cooking, percolating coffee, and the sickly-sweet aroma of burning joss sticks.

I was carried forward by the momentum of the crowd, my eyes searching anxiously for a familiar face — Mark had disappeared as usual. Brothers are seldom attentive escorts at parties.

I felt a soft, warm hand in mind and I looked around.

"Nalini! You look marvellous." She did too in a Laura Ashley dress the colour of a dusky plum.

She smiled — a little tentatively. We hadn't met since the summer.

"How's married life?"

"Very satisfying. Come and sit down. We can have a chat before anyone else arrives."

She led the way to a divan piled with cushions. I looked unbelievingly at the crush of people, wondering how she and Devi proposed to fit another body in. They had obviously made the best use of their small flat at the top of his uncle's house, but at the moment it looked ready to burst at the seams.

"How did your 'O' levels go — as if I need to ask!"

She had taken them in November, just before she married Devi.

She moved her hands expressively and looked embarrassed.

"Well?" I urged.

"I passed them all, except for Physics."

"And now?"

"I'm going to a tech to do 'A' levels — in languages."

"Doesn't Devi mind?"

"Mind!" She seemed astonished. "He has encouraged me to study hard — forced me to sometimes — ever since I left home. *And* he helps with the housework." She looked triumphant as she made the last statement.

One up to Devi, I thought. I wondered what Miss Henley would have said.

"Do you see anything of your parents these days?"

She looked at me squarely. "My mother and grandmother always make me welcome."

I must have shown my surprise because she explained quickly, "It was my grandmother who took my side you know. She's a very wise old lady. She finally persuaded my parents to let me stay and get married."

"And your father?"

She glanced away, "No, I don't see him any more. He goes out when I arrive. 'Typical English girl' he calls me now. I suppose that's what I really want to be," she said. But I could see that it hurt, and I could sympathize.

She turned back to me. "Devi's a Tamil from southern India and my father's a Bengali. I don't suppose you'd understand; we Indians have our own divisions. Besides Devi belongs to a different caste."

I nodded – caste was something I knew quite a lot about.

Nalini's oval face shone with pride as she caught sight of Devi across the room.

"His uncle has been very good to us – renting us this flat as well as giving Devi a job in his business. He didn't even ask my parents for a dowry."

I laughed. "Perhaps it's as well that Devi's an orphan. No mother-in-law trouble for you!"

Nalini didn't join in my laughter. She looked very sober as she said, "I've really been very lucky when you think about it."

Then she smiled. "This isn't Verona, though – it's England; and I'm very glad to be a part of it."

Joan Salvesen was born in South Africa and educated at Victoria Girls' High School and Rhodes University, Grahamstown. She has taught in Cambridge, where she now lives, and has worked in a University library. She has a son and two daughters. Her four published children's books are Uprooted!, Close the Windows Tight, Astrid the Dark-Eyed *and* Journey to the Copper Mountains.

AIMING HIGH

Rosamunde Blackler

"Come here!" my sister Maggie yelled excitedly. "There's a furniture van next door!"

I dashed to the window, and sure enough a big removal van was parked in the small driveway and two men were carrying a wardrobe up the steps to the front door. The house had been empty for quite a few weeks since old Mr and Mrs Brown had left to go and live with their daughter. It was a much bigger house than ours with a lovely garden at the back. As we stood watching at the window a lady about the same age as our Mum came out and said something to the men.

"I wonder if there are any children?" I murmured hopefully. Nobody knew how I longed for a boyfriend. True, there was Dave but since our last row he hadn't asked me out and I couldn't have cared less! I seemed to be falling out with everyone. Stuck up, they called me. And why shouldn't I be stuck up? After all I *was* top of my class and hadn't I just been chosen to play the heroine in the school play? And what sort of a game of tennis did I get with Dave when I always won?

None of them understood that I was aiming high and meant to "go places". I didn't want to spend the rest of my life with people who couldn't see beyond their noses. Even Liz, who'd been my best friend for ages, was becoming a bit of a bore. They didn't understand that I was setting my sights on a world where I'd mix with important people and that I was not going to be held back by small town activities and uninspiring personalities. I included my parents in this for they, too, didn't have a clue about what I wanted to do.

So now you know the sort of mood I was in as Maggie and I stood curiously peeping out of our landing window. The mood hadn't altered much by the next afternoon as I hurried home from school, anxious to see what was going on next door.

"Hi!" called a voice and there on the other side of the hedge stood a young man the spitting image of Paul Glaser. Behind him where the furniture van had been the day before was a bright yellow sports car.

"Hallo," I answered in a dazed sort of way. This just couldn't be true.

"Meet Rob Barton, your next door neighbour," he said smiling kindly and holding out a hand as he walked towards me. "What's a pretty girl like you doing in these parts?"

I looked into his deep brown eyes and fell madly in love. Don't tell me it's impossible. To me he was the most exciting thing that had ever happened and just exactly what I had always imagined my ideal boyfriend to be like. "Please God," I prayed more strongly than I'd ever prayed before, "please let him like me."

It was summer and he was home for three weeks holiday and to help his mother, who was a widow, settle into her new house. I awoke each morning thinking of him and racked my brains to think of ways of running into him. When he and his mother went round inspecting the plants just the other side of the fence at the back of the house I pretended to be picking parsley and mint for my Mum who was cooking in the kitchen.

"Do you like cooking?" asked his mother seeing the bunches in my hand.

"Oh yes," I lied cheerfully, not daring to look behind me at the open kitchen window where my Mum stood whisking eggs for a cake. She knew I'd run a mile to avoid helping her out and that last time she'd asked me to pick something for her I'd said I hadn't time because I had so much homework to do. And as for shopping, which I usually hated, it was quite different when Rob asked me to show him where the shops were. Luckily for me there were masses of little things which his mother kept needing and I made dozens of blissful trips to the town centre. Every time she ran out of tea or bread or suddenly found that she must have more light bulbs or cup hooks or something there was I just waiting round the corner to lead Rob to the right place to get them.

And all the time I was falling more and more in love. It was wonderful striding beside him down the road and I kept my fingers crossed that we'd meet some of my friends from school. I could imagine their envious and incredulous expressions. "Isn't he fabulous – where did you find him?" they'd ask. "I didn't find him – he found *me*," I'd reply. Once Dave passed us in the town. I pretended not to hear his shy "Hallo".

One super sunny day he asked me if I'd like to drive down to the sea for a swim. It was marvellous speeding along in the sports car and I wanted to go on for ever just sitting close to him with the world rushing by. We ate sandwiches on the beach and I told him all about my hopes and dreams for the future: of getting away from home and making a name for myself on radio or TV.

I could scarcely believe my ears when he told me that he worked for a TV company. "I'll put in a good word for you," he said with a laugh.

"Yippee," I yelled at the top of my voice and dashed across the sand into the sea. Rob came running after me and after splashing and fooling around for ages he picked me up in his arms and carried me up to the beach. "Time to go home," he said firmly, and reluctantly I pulled on my clothes and got into the car. It had definitely been the most thrilling day of my life.

After this I ignored my old friends completely. I had better things to do than spend my time with them. I felt that I had already outgrown them and that my life was beginning to go the way it should. I was sure that Rob must have a very important position and be able to help me. Instead of playing the lead in the boring old school play I could see myself on TV being watched by millions of admiring fans. And Rob would be there! "Goodbye, little sweetheart," he said the next day when his holiday was over and gave me a big hug. Sweetheart! I was his little sweetheart!

Everything was unbearable after he'd gone and a few days later I had the most almighty row with Mum. She called me a big-headed little minx. "Right!" I thought. "I'll show you!" I packed some things in a case and caught the next train to London taking the £15 I'd been saving for a new radio. I was pretty scared when I arrived at the huge station and so I got into a taxi and gave the name of the TV company where Rob worked. He would look after his "little sweetheart" when he knew I'd come to him for help. I walked up to the imposing reception desk trying to look like the poised girl friend of a V.I.P I asked to see Rob.

"Rob Barton?" The receptionist looked blank. "What does he do?" she asked. I didn't know. She turned to another woman at the desk. "D'you know

Rob Barton?" The other woman shook her head. They told me I could sit and wait and perhaps I'd see him.

An hour went by. Dozens of people came and went, some chatting and laughing, some looking very important. No one took any notice of me at all as I sat huddled in a corner of a large leather settee. At last Rob stepped out of a lift. A very pretty girl was with him holding his hand. I stood up and walked towards them.

"What on earth are *you* doing here?" Rob asked in utter amazement when he spotted me. A great lump came into my throat and an awful sinking feeling in my stomach.

"I er — er — came to do some shopping," I faltered, "and thought you might be able to show me round."

"You thought WHAT?" he almost gasped. He and the girl stared at each other. They obviously thought I was completely mad. There was a long uncomfortable silence and suddenly I longed for Dave and Liz and Maggie. If they'd been there I might have been able to manage a smile but instead I knew that I was going to cry.

"Sally," Rob said, putting an arm round me, "this pretty little girl lives next door to my mother and I don't think she's ever been away from home before. Let's go and get a cup of tea and then put her on the next train back."

They were very kind to me and Rob said that some time when he was down again staying with his mother he'd give me some tips about getting a job in London. "I'm sure you'll 'go places' one day," he encouraged me with his gorgeous smile, "because you're so enterprising and resourceful." I blessed him for that.

Looking back I can't honestly say that Rob ever did or said anything to make me believe he cared for me. He was just a nice friendly neighbour. It took me weeks to makes things up with Liz and Dave and my other friends and I really felt lonely for a while. I wasn't very good in the school play either. One day I met Rob's mother in the street. "I've just had some wonderful news from Rob," she told me happily. "He's got engaged to a sweet girl. Her name is Sally."

I ran home and picked up the phone. "Is that you, Dave? Can you come round tonight? I need someone reliable to talk to," I said.

Rosamunde Blackler trained as a Youth and Community worker and has worked with young people throughout her career. After working in youth clubs she spent seven years pioneering school counselling in London on a Gulbenkian grant. Her book Fifteen Plus *was published in 1971 and is currently on sale in Japan. After five years as Director of the London YWCA Advisory Service she founded Girls Alone in London Service (GALS). The charity is now known as Alone in London Service and helps both boys and girls.*

A VISIT TO THE HOLY LAND

Kenneth Wood

It was Mark, my brother, who brought the pictures home. That night, when mum and dad were out at the club, he got them out of his pocket and handed them to me. Waiting for gasps of admiration, he sprawled slackly with one leg over the arm of the old easy chair, chewing gum, blowing smoke, and reaching from time to time for the can of beer on the floor by his side. "Whatever your brother goes in for he does well," mum told me once. Just then he was going in for being disreputable, and he was making a good job of it, I thought.

"Take a look at these, Andy! Fresh from Sweden, they are."

Since he'd got the job out there — something to do with oil — he'd brought home all sorts of useless rubbish.

"You'll have to hold them up to the light."

They were slides. Should have been projected on to a screen, but we hadn't a projector. Might have looked better on a screen, I thought. Dirty pictures need to be big perhaps. Anyhow, the blondes who grinned nakedly at me were attractive enough in their way; but you get pictures like that in the newsagents, and not much less on the telly, come to that.

"When you see what some foreigners can produce, it gives you faith in Britain," I told him.

Still, since he left them about, I took them to school to amuse the kids. It was the last week of our

96

school life, and time was dragging even more than usual, so they were passed about with some interest, even though you couldn't see them all that well except in sunlight. We'd lie on the school field at break, on our backs, gaping upwards at the little square transparencies, and hiding them when any teachers came by.

School was to come to an end for me when the public exams started. I'd no chance of being entered for anything except art, and even if I got a certificate for that it wasn't likely to impress old Tom Simson much. He was the butcher who'd taken me on as an apprentice. Built like a heavyweight wrestler he was, with a red face and an ugly scowl. Not the type to appreaciate a bit of landscape or a well-planned lino-cut.

So while the others spent their time revising, we carted desks and chairs about, arranging things for the exam; and in the afternoon we were going to see Mossy Jones's pictures of the Holy Land.

I suppose it was a really big thing for Mossy, to go to those holy places. They said he'd been teaching Religion all his working life, and he probably felt he needed to give some proof he believed in it. So, as they don't burn people at the stake nowadays, he'd gone to the Holy Land.

I'd been taught by him from time to time since I was eleven, when I first went to the comprehensive. I'd drawn a picture of Moses in a basket among the reeds, I remember. He'd put on it, "You draw bullrushes well, but Moses is poor." Later he'd had us for discussion lessons. Just the boys. We'd talked about human relationships, mainly how we felt about girls – our feelings were different from his, but you'd expect that, I suppose. When you're about sixty it must be easy to keep your hands off girls. And easier still when you're dead altogether, come to that.

As we carried the chairs and desks about, we went past the projector in the hall. I stood looking at it. Sandra, my girlfriend, nodded towards a black box on the table.

"His slides must be in there. That's the cassette."

"The what?"

"The cassette. Full of slides. We've got all that stuff at home. God, you are ignorant!"

I was still wondering whether to smack her backside or pull her hair when Mrs Carton, the Senior Mistress, came in and peered around at the chairs and desks. She was a heavy woman, friendly on top, but likely to turn nasty and snap at you. You had to know how far to go with old Ma Carton.

"Sandra."

"Yes, miss?"

"Come along. There's a lot to do."

"Yes, miss."

I pushed the chairs about a bit more. I was alone in the hall.

And it was then that the idea came. It was so quick really that you could hardly call it an idea. I whipped a few slides out of the cassette thing and slipped Mark's girlie ones in instead. I dropped the bits of Holy Land into my pocket and made off.

Mossy was in the corridor talking to Mrs Carton. He was an odd-looking character. Whoever had called him Mossy must have had a bit of genius. He wore a jacket of rough bristly material; he had a straggle of beard and a shapeless moustache; the top of his baldish head was covered with thin down; he was fat and baby-faced – a kind of tree-stump coated with assorted bits of growth. He always had an anxious startled look – like an owl that's just gobbled a clockwork mouse.

"As soon as they are ready, Mrs Carton ... um ... um," I heard him say.

He had a habit of saying, "um ... um". When we were little kids we used to make fun of him for it. When he said, "um ... um", we said "um ... um". We found we could do it with our lips closed, so he couldn't spot us. We soon got tired of it, though; it was less interesting than reading a comic under the desk.

I'd just got back into the classroom and settled in a corner with Sandra, holding hands and watching the rooks wandering near the goalposts on the field, when Mrs Carton came in.

The kids were all lounging about, reading mags or playing cards. One had a radio. Last day at school, after all. Still, when she appeared in the doorway they went quiet suddenly, and I let go of Sandra's hand.

Mrs Carton smiled, but darted suspicious glances about the room. I wondered whether she was going to purr or scratch.

She purred, reproachfully.

"Come on, now, please! The other classes are in the hall. We mustn't keep Mr Jones waiting."

We stood up. She watched us along the passage.

The headmaster, a long, dark, serious man — we'd never seen him smile — stood on the platform at the front of the hall. As he observed us all, he turned his tall thin body from side to side as if he were a robot.

"Williams!" he shouted in a deep echoing voice. "Get out! Go and stand outside my room!"

We watched the little lad leave, stumbling over the feet of those in his row. Mr Fitzhugh would talk to him, would give him a lecture on manners. He was a leisurely headmaster. Not one of the *bend over — thwack-thwack — go away* ones. He would appeal to our better nature. Bit optimistic of him, really.

Mossy was fiddling with the projector in the middle of the room. Desks and chairs were all round him, ready to be set into careful rows for the exams. Tiny traces of sunlight filtered round the edges of the blackouts.

"Hope it breaks down. Then they'll have to let us go home."

"Sh! Sh!"

Sandra scowled at me. She found it difficult, because she was a rather pretty girl. Freckles and fluffy hair; not glamorous, but attractive; and I thought she had the best legs in the fifth year. She mostly wore tight jeans with a heart on one pocket.

Yes, she was attractive all right!

"You'll get us chucked out!"

"Him and his Holy Land. Wish he'd stayed there."

"And now," Fitzhugh said, "we have something that I at least have been waiting to see for some time."

We laughed and sniggered, of course.

He scowled. We stopped. He leaned forward, probing, his big glasses searching us.

Then he straightened himself again.

"I will not tolerate any silliness."

Another scowl.

"As I was saying, I have been looking forward for a long time to seeing the pictures Mr Jones has brought back from the Holy Land. It is certainly very kind of him to give us the opportunity to share his experiences. Thank you. Mr Jones."

We clapped loudly.

"I will now let Mr Jones take my place."

Mossy went on to the platform.

"Well ... um ... um ... what you are going to see is a selection of colour transparencies I ... um ... um

... took on my recent visit to the Holy ... um ... um ... Land. Some of the slides you will see were purchased, but most of them were taken by ... um ... um ... me. With them there is a recorded commentary which I ... um ... um ... have made. I hope therefore that you will keep any questions and comments to the end."

He disappeared from the platform and the lights went out.

I put my arm round Sandra. No point in wasting the whole afternoon.

"No, no!" she said. But would have been surprised if I'd taken any notice. She wriggled and muttered a bit and then gave up.

Funny thing was, Mossy's talk was quite interesting. His voice sounded less silly on the tape, perhaps because there weren't any "um ... ums" and because you couldn't see him, anyhow. If a man looks like a fool, then he'll sound like a fool. But so long as you couldn't see him Mossy sounded quite good. And his pictures were good as well: there were Bedouins with camels and sheep; folk fishing in the Sea of Galilee, and a group of people sitting on that funny Dead Sea you don't sink into because it's so salty. He told us about Lot's wife and how she was changed into a pillar of salt because she turned back to look at Sodom. He said he didn't believe it, though, and this surprised me. I'd always had the idea that because he taught religion he believed all of it. Had to, as part of the job. Like maths teachers, who have to believe their answers are right all the time.

"And now we come to Jericho. You will remember how the soldiers blew their trumpets and the walls fell down. The light was bad for photos that day, so I bought this one."

And up on the screen came one of the Swedish girls.

Well, I'd been right when I'd thought a projector would improve the pictures. Even through a mist of scratches, dust and fingerprints, she looked really something, enlarged.

For a moment or two we were absolutely silent. From the tape, Mossy's voice went on about the walls of Jericho, while we gaped at the girl. Then everyone began to cheer and laugh. We couldn't hear the recording any more, but two more girls appeared before Mossy got round to switching off the tape-recorder. We could hear him blundering about in the darkened room among the furniture. It must have been just about the funniest thing that ever happened in a school hall.

When the lights went on again, the headmaster mounted the platform near the screen and boomed. We went reasonably quiet, except for muttered talk and kids trying to choke back outbursts of laughter. I couldn't see Mossy. Perhaps he'd fled in shame. I suppose most of the folk there thought the pictures were his, anyhow. I wished those I'd nicked weren't still in my pocket. I glanced round, looking for somewhere to hide them. Perhaps I could lean across far enough to drop them behind the radiator? I was just going to try this when Fitzhugh spoke.

"You will now finish arranging the chairs and desks for the examinations. We will leave the projector there for the present."

While he loomed on the platform, like an angry statue, Mrs Carton fussed about, shouting directions. A few other teachers came in. Soon we had the desks in rows, and a chair behind each one. We did it all very quietly. The kids needed time to absorb what had happened, I suppose, after the first hysteria was over.

"Very well!"

We stopped and looked up at him.

"That will do. Thank you. You may now dismiss."

It seemed a bit casual as an end to our school lives. I fancy he would have said something about wishing us well, but nothing seemed suitable, somehow. So we wandered off with our rucksacks and assorted possessions. Sandra turned in the road and gazed at the long low building, all glass and metal, gleaming in the sunlight.

"Come on!" I told her. "Remember Lot's wife."

"It's sad."

"What is?"

"Everything. Leaving school."

"You never learnt anything there. At least, nothing of any use to you."

"That's what's sad. And what happened this afternoon! Somebody must have put those pictures among his. As a joke."

Well, I opened my mouth to tell her, but she went on, "That was an awful thing to do. A really nasty mean trick. Whoever did that ought to be flogged."

We walked slowly down the road, hand in hand, and then turned off into the estate.

After tea I smartened myself up a bit and went round to her place. We'd have the house to ourselves till after seven. Sandra's mum worked stamping books in the library, and her dad was on afternoons at British Chemicals.

I sat beside her on the settee and kissed her. She was watching the kiddy telly: Tarzan and a girl with an afro hair-do were running about some among trees.

"I hope the lions get them," I said.

"They can't do that. Tarzan's back tomorrow."

I kissed her again.

"Switch it off."

"No. It's exciting."

"More exciting than I am?"

"I can switch you on any time."

So I had to watch that mad ape-man running around, but as soon as he'd set things right and trotted away into the jungle, I flung myself at the telly and then caught hold of her. She drew away from me.

"Come on, Sandra!"

"No."

"Oh, come on!"

"Stop it!"

She pushed me away angrily.

"Don't be like that, Andy!"

"Why not?"

"You know why not."

"No, I don't. Why not?"

"We've had all this before."

"Why not, then? You just don't care about me, Sandra. You just don't care."

"You don't try to understand how ..."

"So I don't understand! How can I understand? Other kids our age ... Think ... There's Dave and Joyce ... There's ..."

"Other kids aren't like us."

"Sure they're not! We ought to matter more to one another than ..."

"And when you go on like that you make me ..."

She looked as if she was going to cry. But I blundered on.

"I've a right to go on like that. Are you my girl-friend or not?"

"You mean you want to go off with somebody else?"

"You know I don't want anybody else."

I got my arms round her again.

"Oh, come on! Don't be so ..."

But at the moment she caught sight of one of Mossy's slides. They'd all fallen out of my pocket. There they were, on the floor, near our feet.

"You!" she gasped. "You!"

She stared at me.

"It was you who made him look such a fool! You nicked his pictures! You stole them!"

"Not worth all that much, are they?"

"But they are to *him*. Only time in his life he'll go there. Brings back those pictures. Thinks how wonderful they are. And you do that!"

"Oh, stop making such a silly fuss! They don't matter."

"They might not seem to matter much to you, Andy. But things that matter a lot to some folk don't to others. It's like ..."

She hesitated.

"Anyhow, you'll have to give them back."

"Give them back! That's a laugh! I'll never see him again."

"Then you've stolen them."

"It's not stealing. Not really. Not like nicking things from shops or folk's pockets."

"You stole them. There's no way out of that. And if you don't give them back you're a thief. You'll have to take them back to him. You know where he lives. In Montague Road. A house with a blue door."

She stood up.

"I'll go with you. For a walk."

"I'm not going to be bullied like that."

But I was beginning to feel a bit ashamed.

"I'll decide for myself."

I switched the telly back on. I wasn't going to get anywhere with Sandra just then. On the little screen grown-up men and women threw custard pies at one another. Neither of us laughed.

I was meeting Sandra later at the Club, so I went round by Montague Road. I recognized his car in the drive. Well, I could give them back easily enough. Just drop them through the letter-box and make off. I walked up and down, wondering. Then I hurried up to the door. Just as I got there it opened, and there was Mossy. Perhaps he'd seen me from a window.

He looked even mossier than usual, in a woolly pullover and saggy trousers. I stood in the doorway, clutching the pictures, holding them out to him.

"I've brought these. I took them."

He snatched them from me. Inspected them.

"Ruined! All scratched! Spoilt!"

He glared for a moment and he slammed the door.

I went to the Club and sat in a corner with Sandra, watching the games.

"I took the pictures back."

She kissed me.

"I bet he was grateful!"

"Yes," I said.

She kissed me again.

"Let's play table-tennis," she suggested.

Kenneth Wood was born and educated near Sheffield. He has taught in Cornwall, Blackpool and Manchester, and spent a year at a school in the French Alps. He now teaches at a Sixth Form College. He is married, with two children. He has written radio plays and articles for magazines; but most of his writing has been for teenagers: he has published three teenage novels – Gulls, A Period of Violence, *and* Shadows.